A CON ARTIST
IN PARIS

READ ALL THE MYSTERIES IN THE
HARDY BOYS ADVENTURES:

HARDY BOYS ADVENTURES™

#15 *A CON ARTIST IN PARIS*

FRANKLIN W. DIXON

ALADDIN   New York London Toronto Sydney New Delhi

This book is a work of fiction. Any references to historical events, real people,
or real places are used fictitiously. Other names, characters, places, and events are
products of the author's imagination, and any resemblance to actual events
or places or persons, living or dead, is entirely coincidental.

ALADDIN

An imprint of Simon & Schuster Children's Publishing Division
1230 Avenue of the Americas, New York, NY 10020
First Aladdin hardcover edition September 2017
Text copyright © 2017 by Simon & Schuster, Inc.
Jacket illustration copyright © 2017 by Kevin Keele
Also available in an Aladdin paperback edition.

For information about special discounts for bulk purchases, please contact
Simon & Schuster Special Sales at 1-866-506-1949 or business@simonandschuster.com.
The Simon & Schuster Speakers Bureau can bring authors to your live event.
For more information or to book an event contact the Simon & Schuster Speakers Bureau
at 1-866-248-3049 or visit our website at www.simonspeakers.com.
Series designed by Karin Paprocki
Interior designed by Mike Rosamilia
The text of this book was set in Adobe Carlson Pro.
Manufactured in the United States of America 0817 FFG
2 4 6 8 10 9 7 5 3 1
Library of Congress Control Number 2017943564
ISBN 978-1-4814-9007-8 (hc)
ISBN 978-1-4814-9006-1 (pbk)
ISBN 978-1-4814-9008-5 (eBook)

CONTENTS

FRANK

THE FIRST THING I SAW WHEN I STEPPED
onto the streets of Paris was a giant rat.

"Sweet!" my brother Joe shouted, whipping out his phone to snap a picture of the impossibly large rodent climbing into a sewer in the middle of France's capital.

"I've never seen someone so excited about a rat before," I said. "Or seen a rat wearing a red beret and a burglar mask, for that matter."

Lucky for us, this rat was a five-foot-tall cartoon character running off with a baguette, stenciled on the wall of a *boulangerie*—that's French for "bakery." The artist had layered three different stencils on top of one another so the

1

rat, the baguette, and the beret and mask were all different colors.

"All right! We haven't even been here five minutes and we've already seen a piece by Ratatouille. He's one of the coolest artists working the streets of Paris," Joe gushed.

From his reaction, you'd think we'd just won the tourist lottery.

Our detective dad, Fenton Hardy, had been invited to speak at the annual International Professional Association of Detectives (IPAD) convention, and he'd invited us to tag along for a little sightseeing. We probably could have told all those professional investigators a thing or two about detecting ourselves—I mean, we are the world's foremost underage amateur PIs. Well, at least the foremost in Bayport, our hometown, where we have a well-earned reputation as teenage detectives extraordinaire. Detecting runs in our blood, apparently. IPAD wasn't interested in what Fenton's kids had to say, though, so we got a week off to explore one of Europe's most beautiful cities.

Not even a sleepless nine-hour red-eye flight across the Atlantic could press the snooze button on my excitement level. All that classic art! Architecture! History!

"A brand-new piece by Cosmonaute!" Joe had his phone aimed across the cobblestone street to a simple tile mosaic of a UFO landing on the top story of a brick building that had to be hundreds of years old. "I don't think anyone's even posted this one yet."

The artist had climbed all the way up to the top of the building and glued the square tiles to the wall in the shape of a flying saucer made out of old eight-bit video graphics, like the ones from the very first arcade games.

Joe looked stoked as he uploaded the picture to his Instagram account, adding the hashtags #cosmonaute #streetart #paris and #streetarthuntparis so other street art "grammers" from around the world could see it too.

"I can't believe people come to a city with a world-class museum like the Louvre just to take pictures of cartoon rats and spaceships." I rubbed my confused, jet-lagged eyes. "Here we are in one of the most historic places on earth, surrounded by amazing landmarks, and all my brother wants to see is the graffiti and arcade spaceships."

"It's not just graffiti, dude," he said seriously. "It's street art. People like Ratatouille and Cosmonaute are creating original works of art, *and* they're using the environment around them to tell a story at the same time. There's an international pop art renaissance going on, and Paris is its epicenter."

My brother's head was big enough already without me complimenting him, but I was impressed with how much thought he'd put into it. I was usually the one lecturing him on things like art appreciation!

"I get it, but we're in Paris! Some of the most treasured masterworks ever created are here. Van Gogh, Monet, Picasso, Dali. They all lived and painted right here."

"Well, Snooty McArtFace, Ratatouille painting himself all over Paris turns the whole city into an interactive museum, and you don't have to wait in line or go to a hoity gallery to see it," Joe retorted. "Besides, some people think artists like Le Stylo *are* masters."

"I . . ." I shut up is what I did. "You got me there. I can't talk smack about a guy who got away with turning the most famous clock tower in the world into a smartwatch."

Le Stylo's handle meant "The Pen" in French, and he'd been making international headlines for all the crazy places his outlaw art installations had appeared. Like the time he projected digital numbers and icons over the Big Ben clock tower in London and then changed the sign so it said iBen as a commentary on historical preservation in a tech-driven society.

The whole world was Le Stylo's canvas, and he used it for activism, too. The saying that inspired his name—*the pen is mightier than the sword*—also inspired his art. His antiwar stencils of soldiers wielding his signature feather fountain pen instead of guns had appeared all over the world on government buildings, police headquarters, and even in war zones.

"My favorite is when he used suction cups to scale that mirrored office building in Texas wearing a mirror-covered jumpsuit so no one would see him," Joe said, referencing Le Stylo's protest of a big oil spill the year before.

"Stenciling a flock of oil-covered pelicans crashing into

that big oil CEO's window took talent *and* guts," I agreed, wondering how terrifying it must be to climb a skyscraper like you were Spider-Man. That kind of daredevil stuff was definitely more up Joe's alley.

"I heard he donates all the money from his paintings to charity," Joe shared. "I bet Vincent van Gogh didn't even do that."

"He might have if he hadn't died penniless and unknown," I informed my brother.

"Oh," Joe said, looking up at the sky. "Sorry, Vince, my bad."

"Stylo's definitely got VVG beat in the popularity-while-alive contest," I observed. "It's amazing how someone can turn themselves into just about the world's most popular artist without anyone discovering their real identity."

Le Stylo wasn't just an artist/activist/prankster. He was a mystery. And no one appreciates a good mystery as much as a Hardy boy.

"I can't wait to check out the exhibit with his new work at that Galerie Simone place near the hotel," Joe said. "That's one hoity gallery I don't mind waiting in line for."

It was a different place near the hotel that I was excited to wait in line for. A medieval royal palace filled with over 650,000 square feet of France's most priceless treasures.

BONJOUR, BOYS

2

JOE

OKAY, FOR A STUFFY OLD MUSEUM, the Louvre was pretty epic. The converted palace Frank kept blabbing about took up almost half a mile along the Right Bank of the Seine River. That's what the Parisians call the north side of the river that divides the city in half. The museum may have been historic, but it wasn't entirely old. The gigantic glass pyramid surrounded by triangle-shaped reflection pools in the outdoor square by the entrance gave the place a modern touch I appreciated.

A street cut right through the square, and the whole outdoor part was open to the public without having to buy a ticket, so tons of tourists were taking pictures in front of the pyramid as we walked past. One family was even taking

6

selfies with the security guard next to the little security booth across the square.

"Did you know the Louvre is the largest museum in the world, with over thirty-five thousand objects dating all the way back to prehistoric times?" Frank asked.

"I do now." I chuckled as we cut through the square to our hotel across the street on Rue de Rivoli (that means Rivoli Street).

"Leonardo da Vinci's *Mona Lisa* gets over eight million visitors alone," Frank said, slipping into full tour-guide mode. He'd read so much stuff about Paris before our trip, he could have worked for the French tourism board. "The painting is so valuable, they keep it in an armor-plated steel display case behind multiple layers of impermeable glass. It's practically theft-proof. But part of the reason it's so famous is because it *was* stolen. A handyman actually walked off with it way back in the early 1900s."

"Uh-huh," I mumbled, only half listening.

"When they caught him, he rationalized it by saying that Napoléon Bonaparte, who had been the emperor of France in the early 1800s, soon after the Louvre became a museum, stole it first. Which was actually incorrect, because even though Napoléon had stolen a lot of art during his conquests, the museum had bought that one legally. And now it's the most valuable painting in the world, worth about seven hundred eighty million bucks."

"*Sacré bleu!*" I exclaimed. I thought that meant "sacred

blue"—I didn't speak much French, but I'd seen enough movies to know that's kind of like the French version of "holy cow." I'd totally been kind of zoning out, like I usually do when Frank starts rambling, until he got to the part about 780 million bucks. "Le Stylo's most expensive painting only sold for five hundred thousand dollars. Talk about a million-dollar smile!"

You don't have to be an art scholar to know about the *Mona Lisa*. The painting of a smirking Italian woman still shows up in pop culture over five hundred years later. Even Ratatouille and Cosmonaute had *Mona Lisa* street-art mashups. There was a kind of rivalry between the two street artists, and I'd seen both of their *Mona Lisa* spoofs in my Instagram feed just recently. Cosmonaute's was another simple mosaic made out of square tiles so she looked like a character from an old-school arcade game. Ratatouille's *Monatouille Lisa* looked a lot like the original painting, actually; well, if the original had a smirking rat wearing Ratatouille's signature red beret. They'd both also done versions of Monet paintings, which were pretty cool. Monet was a French Impressionist painter famous for making pictures out of thousands of little dots.

"*Bonjour*, boys," a familiar voice with a Bayport accent greeted us as we walked into the hotel lobby. We turned around to see Bayport's top cop, Chief Olaf, talking to a pudgy older guy holding a fancy carved box. I didn't know who his new friend was, but it sure was odd seeing the chief dressed as a tourist in a floral shirt instead of his normal uniform. Maybe he thought the conference was being held in Hawaii instead of France.

"Hey, Chief!" I said. "Nice fanny pack."

"Thanks, Joe! I got it at . . ." The chief must have figured out I was joking, because he suddenly started growling.

"I think in France it's technically called a *sac banane*," Frank translated helpfully.

"Grrrr," the chief growled again. "It's bad enough you boys make my job harder in Bayport; at least let me enjoy my vacation in Europe."

"Oh, I thought you were here attending the detectives' conference for work, Chief," Frank reminded him. "Don't worry, we won't tell the rest of the department you're taking a vacation on taxpayer money."

"What's French for 'I'm going to lock you up and throw away the key as soon as we get back to Bayport'?" he deadpanned to Frank.

"Hmm, I'm not sure," Frank said, checking the translation app on his phone. "I think it's, *Je vais vous . . . ohhh*."

"Good one, Chief," I said. "You're catching on."

"*Touché*, as the French say." Chief Olaf beamed proudly. "It's a shame about your dad's flight getting canceled. I just hope that storm lets up in time for him to make it for his lecture in a couple of days."

"Us too," Frank said. "Dad's really been looking forward to it."

Our pops had been wrapping up a case and was supposed to fly out that morning, but all the flights after ours had been grounded.

"I figure it's my job to keep an eye on you boys until he gets here," the chief said pointedly. "You stir up enough trouble in little ol' Bayport; we don't need you causing an international incident with a whole other country."

I'm not sure I agreed with the chief's definition of trouble, but our investigations did have a habit of stepping on the police's toes back home.

"No worries, Chief," I assured him. "We really are here on vacation."

"You better be, because if you think I'm a grump, wait till you meet Chief Inspector Devereux." Chief Olaf nodded to a tall, stern-looking man talking to a group of guests across the lobby.

"*Oui, l'inspecteur* has a ferocious reputation, which I, for one, take great comfort in," interjected the pudgy Frenchman.

"Joe and Frank Hardy, meet Monsieur Plouffe," the chief said, introducing us.

"It's a pleasure to meet you, sir," Frank said, shaking his hand. "Are you one of the detectives here for the IPAD conference too?"

"Ah, *non*, I may be the only guest at the hotel who is not," Plouffe said in his thick French accent.

"Monsieur Plouffe is a collector of historical French art and antiques," the chief filled us in.

"*Oui*, and I just made a rather extraordinary purchase for my collection. So I thought, where safer to keep it during the remainder of my stay in Paris than the safe in a hotel full of the world's best police detectives?" Plouffe gestured to the IPAD guests milling about the lobby.

He held the carved box out for us to examine, then opened it so reverently I thought rays of golden light might come flying out while angels started singing. They didn't, but the contents were pretty impressive.

"Whoa!" Frank's mouth dropped open. "That fountain pen must be over two hundred years old. And it looks like it's solid gold, even the nib."

"Very good! You know your history," Plouffe complimented Frank as he lifted the pen to the light. It was one of those old-fashioned pens from way back in the days when you had to keep dipping the pen in a bottle of ink to write. I may not know a lot about antique pens, but I could tell this one was special. It was embossed with vines wrapped around a stag's antlers, and it had the initials N.B. carved in fancy script on the flattened gold tip (that's the part Frank called the nib).

"It was Napoléon Bonaparte's, seized from the desk of a vanquished foe," Plouffe continued, setting the pen back in the box next to a jar of dried ancient black ink. "The emperor used this very pen to write his last letters from exile before his death in 1821."

Napoléon was a big deal in France, and everywhere else

in the world too, for that matter. I may not be a history nerd like Frank, but even I knew that Napoléon was one of the most famous military leaders of all time.

"That, boys, is the most expensive pen you'll ever see," the chief said proudly, as if it was his own.

"Nine hundred and fifty thousand euros, to be exact," said Plouffe as he closed the case.

"That's over a million dollars," Frank gasped.

"And worth every penny for someone who values the preservation of France's past as much as I do," Plouffe said. "It sat on the desk of an emperor, and when I return to my château in the countryside, it will sit on mine."

"That's a really cool pen, Mr. Plouffe, but for a million big ones, I'll stick with my trusty ballpoint Bic." I tried to stifle a yawn.

"You kids look about as tired as I feel," said the chief. "I say we all call it a night."

We'd somehow lucked out and had a room on the top floor overlooking the Louvre, but Frank and I were so tired we both passed out before we got a chance to check out the view.

I was in the middle of a dream about Napoléon fighting in battle when I realized those weren't cannons I was hearing, they were fireworks. And they were coming from outside our window.

"Is this how they wake up every day in France?" I groaned, squinting through bleary eyes to see the 5:01 A.M. on my phone.

"Sumpnwerdsgonon," Frank mumbled from his bed. Or at least that's what it sounded like.

"English, bro," I said.

He cleared his throat and tried a second time. "Something weird is going on."

We stumbled out of our beds and over to the window to see a huge display of red and blue fireworks exploding over the Louvre, illuminating the huge sign that now hung down the side of the seventy-foot-tall glass pyramid in front of the museum.

"Uh, that wasn't there yesterday, was it?" I asked.

"Uh-uh," he replied, mouth agape.

The sign read BONJOUR, INSPECTEURS! above a thirty-foot-tall Le Stylo–style stencil caricature of the *Mona Lisa* holding Le Stylo's signature feathered pen as if she had just finished drawing herself. Below that were the words, NE ME BLÂMEZ PAS. NAPOLÉON LA VOLÉ EN PREMIER.

Frank was already typing away into his French to English translation app.

"Don't blame me," he read. "Napoléon stole it first."

THE VANISHING SMILE

3

FRANK

BY THE TIME WE'D MADE IT DOWN TO the lobby, detectives in their pajamas had started pouring out of the hotel and across the street like a half-dressed herd of frantic international investigators. I noticed Monsieur Plouffe, the art collector, among them. A series of booms echoed from the hotel roof as we followed, showering everyone in French-flag-colored red and blue confetti shot from a confetti cannon somewhere on the hotel roof.

"I think we've just become part of Le Stylo's newest stunt," Joe called as the confetti-covered detectives reached the foot of the Louvre pyramid.

I looked up at the towering drawing of the *Mona Lisa* smirking with the outlaw artist's pen in her hand.

A funny-looking tiny European car zipped into the square, and out hopped Chief Inspector Devereux, already in a well-tailored suit and on the job at the break of dawn. Devereux marched toward the outdoor security guard booth across the square, where a baffled security guard stood looking up at the sign, scratching his head.

"*Je veux voir la caméra de sécurité de la* Mona Lisa," Devereux shouted at the guard in French. "*Maintenant!*"

"He's going to look at the security footage," one of the investigators translated. Everyone surged forward after him, eager to know what would happen next.

"Stay back!" Devereux yelled in English at the hotel guests.

They didn't. Since both the pyramid and the security booth were outside in the public square, there was nothing Devereux could do to stop a group that large from going anywhere they wanted. About fifty pajama-clad detectives jostled for position to get a look through the security booth's open door.

I was able to slip through the scrum right to the front of the crowd. The booth was only big enough for him and the guard to fit inside, but most of us had a clear view over Devereux's shoulder or through the window.

The video monitor flickered to life in the security booth, flipping through different angles until it reached the display with the *Mona Lisa*.

And the empty frame where the most valuable painting in the world should have been.

NOW YOU SEE IT . . .

4

JOE

SO MUCH FOR THE *MONA LISA* BEING theft-proof! Her famous smile was gone right along with the rest of her.

The detectives who could see gasped in unison and passed the news along to their colleagues behind them. Chief Inspector Devereux was busy yelling a lot of unhappy-sounding things in French. The security guard yelled something else into his walkie-talkie, and a minute later another security guard appeared on camera, running into the room where the *Mona Lisa* was displayed.

But as soon as the guard ran past the turnstiles meant to rope the painting off from the public and stepped in front of the empty frame, the frame wasn't empty anymore! Mademoiselle Mona Lisa had suddenly reappeared!

This time Inspector Devereux gasped right along with everyone else as the baffled security guard checked to make sure he wasn't hallucinating. Nope. The painting really was there. Something else was there as well—a faint flicker of light on the back of the security guard's black jacket. It didn't take long for the news to spread.

I flashed back through the conversation Frank and I had yesterday about Le Stylo. I looked at my brother and could tell he was doing the same. Frank and I may not be twins, but we do have a brotherly connection that's kind of uncanny sometimes.

"Big Ben!" we both blurted in unison.

Everyone turned and stared at us like we were crazy.

"It's a 3-D projection," I said. "Le Stylo used a trick like this to make it look like Big Ben in London had turned into a digital clock."

Inspector Devereux peered out of the booth to give me a cold stare. "Who are you?"

Chief Olaf stepped forward in his bathrobe and replied for us before we got the chance. "Joe and Frank Hardy. Fenton Hardy's boys."

Devereux made a French-sounding grunt and promptly ignored us.

"There's got to be a projector of some kind hidden in one of the poles that ropes off the painting," Frank insisted. "You can see the image of the blank frame on the security guard's back."

"And there." I pointed at the screen. I was now leaning pretty far into the booth. "See how the edges of the frame go dark when the guard moves around?"

Before Devereux could reply, the guard in the booth shouted over the walkie-talkie to the guard in the room. The guard inside turned toward the ropes and instantly had to cover his eyes. He leaned down so that he was staring straight into the black cap of the center pole.

The security guard stood up. Smiling, he held a tiny black pocket projector up to the camera. The theft of the painting was nothing but a hoax, and the *Mona Lisa* was right where she always had been.

There was some relieved nervous laughter from some of the detectives. Frank didn't laugh, though, and neither did I. Le Stylo had been known to provoke the authorities before, but his stunts usually had a larger message, and this seemed like a pretty risky prank just to needle the police. What was the bigger picture?

"Everyone back to the hotel," Devereux ordered, glaring at the crowd of half-dressed detectives. "Or I will arrest all of you for public indecency. We need to set up a crime scene, and you are simply in the way."

The chief inspector looked directly at us when he said this last part.

"Come on, boys," Chief Olaf encouraged, putting a hand on each of our shoulders. Neither Frank nor I budged, though. We were studying the sign on the pyramid too intently. There was the huge caricature of the *Mona Lisa* holding Le Stylo's signature pen, drawn in Le Stylo's signature style, and below that the sentence Frank had translated as, "Don't blame me. Napoléon stole it first."

"But Napoléon didn't steal the *Mona Lisa*," Frank said, coming to the same conclusion I had.

"I thought I told you to go back to—" Devereux started to say, but I tuned him out as I keyed in on the fountain pen in Mona Lisa's hand.

"Um, I think there's something else Napoléon did steal," I said, looking over at Monsieur Plouffe, who must have had the same realization, because . . .

"*Oh mon Dieu!*" he blurted, and a second later he was sprinting back across the square toward the hotel, his robe billowing out behind him as he went.

"Pretending to steal the *Mona Lisa* wasn't a hoax . . . ," Frank declared.

"It was a distraction!" I finished his sentence for him and took off running after Plouffe.

The whole mob of pajamaed detectives took off after us, leaving Devereux standing at the foot of the Louvre pyramid, wondering what had just happened.

GOSSIPING GUMSHOES

5

FRANK

WE CAUGHT UP WITH PLOUFFE AS he ran back inside the hotel and past the reception desk to the manager's office, where the hotel safe was. He yanked on the locked doorknob and turned to the befuddled manager, who had just arrived for the morning shift and didn't seem to have any idea what was going on.

"*Ouvrez la porte! Ouvrez la porte! Ouvrez-la tout de suite!*" Plouffe yelled at him. I understood enough French to know Plouffe was telling him to open the door.

The manager fumbled with his keys while Plouffe bounced up and down anxiously. He shoved the manager out of the way as soon as he found the right key and flung the door open himself. He stumbled back instantly, coughing as a cloud of gray smoke billowed out.

"*C'est un feu!*" the manager cried.

The smoke stung my nostrils as it washed over us. *Feu* meant "fire," but . . .

"It doesn't smell like fire," I said, covering my face with my shirt and trying to wave the smoke away.

"And I don't see any flames," Joe coughed.

The manager fumbled for a switch on the wall and an overhead fan whirred into motion, blowing enough of the smoke out the door for us to see inside the windowless office.

The smoke seemed to be coming up from the floor behind the antique desk on the other side of the room.

"The safe!" Plouffe moaned, running across the room with us on his heels and leaning over the desk, the color draining from his face as he stared at the floor where the safe was.

And by "was," I mean used to be. Because the safe had been replaced by a big hole in the floor. Plouffe's newly purchased million-dollar *stylo* was gone along with it, whisked away into a smoky tunnel under the hotel.

Plouffe stood there like a stunned fish, silently opening and closing his mouth, unable to speak.

"What's below this building?" Joe asked the manager, who ran beside us and peered over the desk.

"The safe has disappeared into the sewers!" he gasped.

I stared down into the gaping hole. I waved away the last of the smoke wafting up from a small canister sitting in a pile of rubble on the damp tunnel floor—the smoke bomb the thief had left behind to obscure his escape route.

"Le Stylo has stolen my *stylo*!" Plouffe clutched his chest as if he might have a heart attack. Then he clutched me. "We must get it back!"

"I'm sorry, Monsieur Plouffe, but there are hundreds of miles of crisscrossing sewer tunnels and ancient catacombs hidden under the streets of Paris," I coughed through my shirt. "By the time the rest of the smoke clears, the trail will be stone cold."

The smoke remained thick in the unventilated tunnel beyond, and I figured the thief had dropped a few more smoke bombs along the way.

"Talk about a distraction," Joe said, looking down at the rubble. "With everyone across the street gawking over the pyramid and all those fireworks and the confetti cannon going off, he would have had the time and cover he needed to bust through the floor from below without anyone hearing."

"Get the children out of here," Devereux's voice growled from the doorway.

"Children?!" Joe snapped back. "I bet we've solved more mysteries than you have."

I put my hand on Joe's arm to keep him from boiling over.

"What my brother means, sir," I backtracked, "is that we're very familiar with Le Stylo's MO and may be able to help piece together—"

"Help? Me?" He staggered back, hand on his chest. "Ha! Out. Now. Before I arrest you for tampering with a crime scene."

"What are you going to do to find my pen, Inspector?" Plouffe demanded, interrupting just in time to prevent Joe from saying something we both might regret.

"There you are!" Chief Olaf exclaimed after forcing his way into the room through the throng of detectives trying to get a peek at their second crime scene of the morning. "I thought I told you two to keep a low profile."

The chief dragged us back out into the lobby, where about fifty detectives from all over the world, most of them still in their pajamas, were rapidly trading speculations about how Le Stylo had pulled off the Louvre stunt.

"The Louvre has some of the best security in the world. How did Le Stylo manage to scale a seventy-foot-glass pyramid surrounded by cameras and drop a sign over the side without being seen?" a tall detective with a Middle Eastern accent asked.

The consensus seemed to be that no one had a clue.

"Ah! It's the security footage from the Louvre!" a British-accented detective I'd heard people call Stucky exclaimed. "My friend on the Paris force sent it to me. They're as clueless about what happened as we are."

The chief tightened his grip on our arms and yanked us toward the elevator.

"Might as well share it with everyone. We're all detectives

here, and fifty heads are better than one," we heard Stucky say behind us.

A second later phones started buzzing all over the lobby as the detectives messaged the video around. The elevator door had just dinged open when the chief's phone buzzed as well.

"I bet that's the video!" I said.

"Please!" Joe added as we both looked up at him with our best non-trouble-making puppy-dog eyes.

"Arghh, fine!" he relented, pulling out his phone. "But only because I want to see it too."

We could already hear people delivering a rush of commentary as they watched the footage.

"It's like he's invisible. The cameras outside show nothing but a shimmer of light along the side of the glass. How is that possible?" one detective wondered.

"It's the same from the angle inside the pyramid. It looks like there's a patch of glass inching upward, but you'd never even notice if you weren't specifically looking for something amiss," added another.

"I've never seen anything like this," chimed in Stucky. "Is this Le Stylo fellow a magician?"

Joe, the chief, and I stared intently at the pyramid on the screen as the footage played. The time stamp on the video said 4:30 A.M., and it was still dark. Without the fireworks illuminating the square, the whole thing was lit by the decorative glow of orange interior lights reflecting back and forth off the triangle-shaped pools surrounding the pyramid.

From the footage, it really did seem like the thief was a ghost. He looked nearly transparent. There was a shimmer of light slowly moving up the pyramid, but that was about it until a few more flashes of light twinkled off the sign as it was dropped over the other side. But you could barely see that, either.

"You can't even see the sign, because the material's transparent and the words and the *Mona Lisa* stencil are both reflective silver," I observed. "The orange light from the glass pyramid and the pools of water just reflect right back off it like camouflage."

A lightbulb seemed to go on over Joe's head. "What if it wasn't just the sign that was reflective?"

A second lightbulb suddenly went on over mine. "It wouldn't be the first time Le Stylo used a mirror suit to climb a building unseen."

"And with the reflection pools surrounding the glass pyramid reflecting the pyramid back at him from every angle, he would have become practically invisible," Joe said.

The chief looked from me to Joe. "What are you boys talking about?"

By this time, some of the other detectives had begun to gather around as well.

"I guess most detectives aren't street-art aficionados," Joe said, looking rather smug.

"Le Stylo made a special flexible suit covered from head to toe in hundreds of tiny mirrors for a stunt in Texas last year," I explained. "When the suit is worn against another reflective surface without anything else to break up the person's silhouette, they blend right into the background so you almost can't even tell they're there."

"Brilliant!" commented Stucky in his British accent. "But how did he climb the blasted thing in the first place? Is he Spider-Man?"

Joe smiled. "Sort of. He used suctions cups on his hands and feet to climb a glass skyscraper as part of the same Texas stunt."

"Splendid work, chaps. It looks like the grown-ups aren't the only detectives in the building after all," Stucky declared. "You must go and tell the chief inspector you cracked the first part of the case."

Both Joe and I looked at Chief Olaf, who nodded his approval. "Come on." The chief gestured toward the inspector.

Unfortunately, Devereux was not impressed. We hadn't even made it all the way through our theory when he cut us off. "You can leave the detecting to the professionals."

"Now wait a second there, Inspector," the chief jumped to our defense. "I think you should hear the boys out—"

"As I said, Mr. Olaf, leave the detecting to the professionals," Devereux interrupted. "Now, good day."

"It's *Chief* Olaf, and you—" But the chief didn't get a chance to finish, because Devereux simply turned his back and walked away. Chief Olaf got even redder than he does when he's angry at us and stomped off in the opposite direction, grumbling to himself about being called unprofessional.

"I take that as the chief's approval of our ongoing

independent investigation," Joe said, staring daggers at Devereux's back.

"We'll show that guy how the professionals in Bayport do it," I concurred.

One of the things we'd learned from our dad is that a keen set of ears is often a detective's best weapon, so I turned mine to the lobby full of IPAD investigators. The gossiping gum-shoe rumor mill had continued to pick up steam, and the current topic of conversation seemed to be Le Stylo's identity.

"I think the theory that it's a group of different people holds the most water," a woman with a Boston accent said. "It would explain how Le Stylo is able to pull off such complex stunts in so many different global locales."

"My money's on that Parisian philanthropist art collector fellow, Cyril Brune," Stucky interjected. "He's filthy rotten rich and they say he's one of these extreme sports daredevils, travels around the world doing daredevil stunts for fun."

"I've heard the same rumors," Joe told me with a frustrated sigh. "And there are a ton more, but there's no real evidence for any one of them."

"So where should we start?" I asked.

"I don't know, but there's one thing that's really bugging me about this case, and I don't mean Chief Inspector Snooty," he said. "This crime just doesn't fit Le Stylo's profile."

I looked at him skeptically. "A high-profile public stunt that provokes the authorities using the same exact technology Le Stylo has used before doesn't fit his profile?"

"I guess," Joe conceded. "But he's never stolen anything before. It's out of character. His installations usually make a comment about society or protest some kind of injustice. He's an activist, not a thief."

"Not until now, at least," I pointed out.

"Yeah, I guess," he said, looking over at Monsieur Plouffe, who sat nearby, as distraught as ever, with the phone to his ear.

"*S'il vous plaît, appelez-moi immédiatement si vous entendez quelque chose de vos contacts, Simone,*" he pleaded in French.

My French wasn't good enough to pick up what he was saying, and there was too much background noise to use my translator app, but the name Simone rang a bell.

I walked over as soon as he hung up the phone.

"Excuse me, Monsieur Plouffe, but can I ask who you were speaking to?"

"The art dealer through whom I purchased Napoléon's pen," he said dejectedly. "I had hoped she might be able to help the police with their investigation, but she has nothing to offer besides her sympathy."

"You said her name was Simone?" I prompted.

"Yes. Simone Lachance," he said. "She owns a number of galleries around Paris. There's one not far from here, I believe, but it is contemporary art, in which I have little interest."

"Galerie Simone?" Joe asked, wide-eyed.

"*Oui*, you have heard of it?" Plouffe asked, surprised.

"We sure have," I told him. "That's where Le Stylo's new exhibit is."

THE LUCKY LADY

6

JOE

LE STYLO'S STUNT WAS GOOD FOR BUSI-
ness at Galerie Simone, that's for sure. It was
only two o'clock in the afternoon, but the hip
Left Bank gallery was packed. So packed we
had to wait in line for half an hour before we
reached the ginormous security guard. The guy was so
big you couldn't even see the stool he sat on, and his old-
fashioned driving cap was pulled so low you couldn't see
his eyes, either, just ominous shadows. We were about to
follow the couple in front of us inside when he snapped
the velvet rope closed.

"Um, *pardon, monsieur, s'il vous plaît*..." Frank fumbled
in French, but the guard didn't wait for him to finish.

"If you want to see art you can afford, there's a comic

book store across the street," he rumbled with an impossibly deep French accent.

"Hey, how do you know what we can afford?" I bluffed. "This gallery is open to the public, and we want to come in."

The guard growled, and I don't mean a normal grumpy-person growl like Chief Olaf's. This one practically made my toes vibrate. The stool groaned under his weight as he began to stand. Luckily, he only made it halfway when someone laughed behind us.

"Oh, come on, Luc," the man said in perfect English with just a hint of a French accent. He was about half the size of Luc the Ginormo Security Guard, but he was so fit and sharply dressed he looked like he'd stepped right out of *GQ* magazine. The sparkling high-tech dive watch on his wrist probably cost as much as one of Le Stylo's paintings.

"Most people in there can't afford it either, and you know it. Let the young gentlemen in," the man continued.

Luc growled again, but he did as he was told. I was about to say something to rub it in our friend Luc's face, but the sound of his knuckles cracking made me think better of it, so I hurried past him instead.

Our rescuer gave us a wink and strode across the room to shake someone's hand before we had a chance to thank him.

"Remind me to get rich enough to buy a watch like that," I said to Frank.

"Remind me never to cross paths with Luc again," he retorted.

"Wow, there's a ton of people here," I said, eyeing all the people crowding around Le Stylo's paintings, pretty much all of them gossiping about the morning's crime.

Le Stylo's work wasn't the only art in the gallery, but it was the only art getting any attention. As we canvassed the place, we walked past a small photography exhibit in the back, documenting the Paris street-art scene. None of the pictures showed Le Stylo's pieces, but there were lots of less famous street artists like Cosmonaute, and a bunch of pictures featuring Ratatouille's work too. One really cool photo showed a close-up of Ratatouille in his red beret stenciled over the window of a camera shop, holding a vintage camera to his eye. The way the photographer framed it, it looked like Ratatouille was the one taking the picture of himself in the window.

"Georges St. Denis," Frank read the photographer's signature aloud from the bottom of the frame.

The only other people in Georges St. Denis's exhibit were a group of men and women gathered around a table with a fancy cheese plate. They looked like artists themselves, and from the way they were talking, not everybody at Galerie Simone was impressed with Le Stylo's work.

A short, mousy-looking guy with bright red hair, paint-splattered sneakers, and a camera around his neck seemed to be the ringleader. I didn't hear the last thing he'd said, but a tall blond woman in coveralls was nodding vigorously.

"You are correct," she said with what I think was a Dutch accent. "His technique, meh, it is okay, but there is no depth to it. The message is splashed obviously all over the surface."

"It is of little surprise he turned to theft. He has been stealing from other artists for years," the redheaded guy agreed, munching on a piece of cheese.

He looked vaguely familiar, but I couldn't quite put my finger on it. Like maybe he reminded me of someone famous, but I couldn't think of who.

"He bought his fame with marketing stunts," he continued, waving his hand dramatically at the photographs displayed behind him. "Just look at the work of the other artists illustrating the streets of Paris. Cosmonaute, for example, and Ratatouille, who is perhaps the most underrated. These are the true artists of the *révolution de l'art de la rue.*"

I was tempted to say something in Le Stylo's defense, but Frank grabbed my arm.

"I bet that's Simone Lachance." He nodded across the gallery to a pretty woman with jet-black hair highlighted by a silver streak that fell over one eye. She tucked a strand of hair behind her ear as she showed off one of Le Stylo's paintings, exposing a glimmering diamond stud. *La chance* meant "luck" in French, and from Simone's appearance, she'd had her share.

The fancy French proprietress was in full schmooze mode as many of the gallery's richest-looking patrons clamored for her attention, gathering around the painting to hear what she had to say.

"Should we eavesdrop?" asked Frank.

"*Oui, oui,*" I agreed.

We were a few feet away when her cell phone rang and she excused herself. We quickly turned our backs so it looked like we were studying one of the paintings.

"Let's intercept her on her way back and see if we can get her to answer a few questions," I suggested.

As soon as she clicked off, Frank moved in. "*Bonjour, madame, parlez-vous anglais?*"

She looked at him like he was from another planet instead of another country.

"Of course I speak English. My galleries do business all over the world, and my contacts in New York and London are too lazy to learn proper French. Although it's probably for the best. They just botch it when they try. What do you want? As you can see, we are very busy."

"Well, um, we're visiting with our high school and, um, doing a project on the contextualized social activism in Le Stylo's public art installations . . . for our art history class," Frank improvised, "and we were at the Louvre where he pulled that stunt this morning. . . ."

"Ach, that." She grimaced. "What a mess. I've had police and journalists harassing me all day. As if I know who he is."

"But you're the only art dealer in the world he lets sell his work. How can you not know who he is?" I asked. If anyone had known, I'd figured it was her.

She gave an annoyed wave of her hand. "Unfortunately, the police think the same thing. I wish I did know so I could give him a piece of my mind, but a mysterious assistant who calls himself Mr. Nib arranges everything by e-mail, and the paintings are delivered to me anonymously."

"Surely you must pay somebody when his paintings sell. There's got to be a money trail," Frank prodded.

She gave him a suspicious look. "There's no money trail to follow, because Le Stylo insists that the proceeds from every sale are sent straight to charity. Mr. Nib tells me where to send the money, and I send it. What kind of school project did you say this was?"

"Why do you think he picked you to represent his work?" Frank ignored her and pressed ahead with the questions. She stepped back like he'd slapped her.

"Ha! Isn't it obvious? No one else in Paris could have driven the global market and legitimized his work within the art world as I have. He is much smarter than most of these other 'street artists,'" she said with finger quotes, giving a dismissive look toward the photography exhibit at the back of the gallery. "Before this Mr. Nib of his asked me to broker his sales, his *masterpieces* were considered little more than high-concept vandalism by the cretins with the real money."

We had Simone Lachance on a roll, and I figured I'd better keep pressing her before she shut the interview down. She seemed like a pretty shrewd operator, so . . .

"Kind of a strange coincidence that Le Stylo decided to steal the pen you just sold to another one of your clients," I observed casually, hoping to fluster her into letting her guard down.

"Who are you?" she demanded. "You're way too young to be police or insurance investigators, but if I did not know better, I'd say this was an interrogation."

"We're just staying at the same hotel as Monsieur Plouffe is all," Frank explained, trying to defuse her. "He was showing off the pen last night and was very distressed this morning after it was stolen."

"Plouffe." She said his name like it was a bad odor. "Another cretin. This mess is the last thing I needed. You can be certain I will be telling Mr. Nib exactly what I think about his Le Stylo throwing me under the *autobus*. I have many other clients and a reputation to protect."

"You have to admit, the stunt hasn't been half-bad for business," I needled, looking around the packed gallery.

"I suppose it hasn't," she said, narrowing her eyes at me. "Not that it does me much good. He, or she, or whatever Le Stylo is, makes me donate my normal commissions to charity as well. 'Social activism.' Ha! Rather hypocritical in light of recent events, no?"

I frowned. She had me there.

"Why bother selling his work at all if you aren't getting paid?" Frank asked.

"Normally, representing him *is* good for business," she replied. "The art world looks to me to tell them what is worth collecting. It would not have done for another gallery to make Le Stylo a star."

Simone turned to leave, then stopped and turned back.

"And I wouldn't feel too terrible for your poor Monsieur Plouffe. He made absolutely sure that pen was insured for considerably more than he paid. I suspect he'll be earning quite a handsome return on his investment."

We hadn't been expecting that. Was there a secret silver lining to the theft of the golden pen that could turn Plouffe's misfortune into a fortune? Could the bereaved collector possibly be the architect behind his own distress?

Simone Lachance walked off, leaving us alone to consider Plouffe's plight in front of the largest Le Stylo installation in the gallery. It was an actual eight-foot-tall slice of brick wall torn out of the side of a building. Almost the entire thing was blank except for the top and the bottom. A little girl was stenciled at the bottom, holding an umbrella and looking up at the silhouettes of bomber planes flying across the top. Only instead of bombs, they were dropping Le Stylo's signature fountain pens. The price tag on the bottom said 400,000 EUROS.

"Do you like it?" a familiar smooth voice with a light French accent asked from behind us. "I just bought it."

My mouth dropped open as I looked from the ginormo painting's ginormo price tag to the well-dressed guy who had helped save us from Luc the Ginormo Security Guard.

"I'm afraid our ill-mannered friend at the door didn't take the trouble to introduce us." He extended the hand with the gazillion-dollar dive watch. "My name is Cyril Brune."

ALTERED EGOS

7

FRANK

STARED UP AT CYRIL BRUNE, THE RICH DARE-devil philanthropist . . . and one of the men rumored to secretly go by the alter ego Le Stylo.

"Um, Frank," I said, shaking his hand.

"And Joe," my brother added.

"Hardy," we said together.

He focused on the installation in front of us, biting his lip as he stared at it.

"Well, Frank and Joe Hardy, what do you think?" he asked again. He looked at us like he was genuinely interested in our opinion, but I think we were both still too shocked by the price tag to formulate a response.

"Oh, don't worry, I didn't pay face value for it," he said

when he saw us gawking. "I paid one hundred fifty thousand euros more."

"Okay, math might not be my best subject," Joe said, trying to process what Cyril Brune had just told us, "but . . . what?!"

"And, um . . . why?!" I added.

Cyril laughed. "Why not? I can afford it, and it all goes to charity anyway. Driving up the price of Le Stylo's work simply means the rich fools like me who are willing to pay for it are forced to give more to people who need it."

"Wow, Mr. Brune, that's really cool of you," I said, my brain still spinning, trying to wrap itself around what it must be like to have so much money you could pretty much just give away fortunes on a whim.

"Oh, just plain Cyril is fine. The art world puts on enough airs," he said, returning his gaze to the brick wall. "To be honest, I'm not even sure how much I like this one. Le Stylo does tend to recycle his own imagery, and the only thing that makes this one special is that it still remains on a part of the original wall."

"No offense, Cyril, but if you don't like it, why did you pay five hundred fifty thousand euros for it?" Joe asked.

"Oh, I didn't say I didn't like it. I said I wasn't sure. This may sound funny coming from a well-known art collector, but I've never been very confident when it comes to judging art," he confessed sadly. "What I am sure I like is Le Stylo's business model, if you can call giving away money a business model, that is. Le Stylo's got guts, and he puts his money where his brush is. Paying a premium for his work simply gives me a chance to pay the message forward."

"That's really admirable of you, Cyril," I said.

Cyril shrugged off the compliment humbly (or at least as humbly as someone in a few-thousand-dollar sport coat can shrug) and then leaned in with a devilish little grin. "Besides, it rankles my friend Simone to know how much additional commission she isn't earning."

"You know," Joe said tentatively, "some people think you're the one putting his money where his brush is."

Cyril smiled.

"Oh, those ridiculous rumors that I'm Le Stylo? I wish!" He looked around the gallery wistfully. "Sadly, I'm not much of an artist myself, and I have a letter from the dean of my art college asking me not to return to prove it, so I do my best to support those who are. I haven't picked up a paintbrush since I flunked out; now I pick up my wallet instead. I may not have been lucky enough to be gifted with talent, but I was gifted a huge inheritance. May as well put it to good use, no?"

He was about to add something else when he looked up at the door and his face sagged. "Not again."

Following his gaze, we saw a small mob of reporters and TV cameras through the window, trying to push their way inside past Luc.

"They've been chasing after me ever since the news broke

about that awful Louvre prank this morning. I have to admit, those stupid rumors about me being Le Stylo were a little more fun before this whole disaster. Now they're just going to paint Le Stylo as a villain."

"After what he did this morning, he kind of is the villain," I said.

"And a thief, from the looks of it," Joe mumbled, giving a disappointed kick at the floor.

"Maybe. Maybe not," Cyril said matter-of-factly, casting another glance at the window, where the TV cameras were jostling for position to get shots of him. "Darn. They've spotted me. No sneaking by them now."

Cyril's frown suddenly turned upside down as he looked at us. "Would you boys mind doing me a huge favor?"

"Um, I don't know what kind of favor we could possibly do for you, Cyril, but sure," I said.

"I'm going to step back to the restroom for a minute," he said. "If you boys could tell those newshounds out front that you saw Cyril Brune slip out the back door, I'd certainly appreciate it."

"Sure," Joe agreed, "but why not just go ahead and actually slip out the back door on your own first?"

"Because there isn't one," he said with a grin. "But by the time they realize that, I'll have already slipped out the front."

"No problem," both Joe and I agreed at once. That was our kind of plan.

He gave us a big warm smile. "Tell you what, I'm having

a little get-together at my place tonight. I'd be honored if you stopped by."

Joe and I looked at each other. We weren't about to turn down that offer.

"Fantastic. It's settled, then. Where are you staying?"

"Grand Hotel du Louvre," I told him.

"Lovely. I'll send a car around this evening." And with that he strode toward the back of the gallery.

His plan worked perfectly. Luc gave us a confused glance when we told the mob of reporters Cyril had slipped out the back, but he didn't say anything.

We got back to the hotel a few hours later to find the IPAD detectives buzzing with gossip. Turns out there had been a new development in the case since we'd left the gallery: packages containing super-valuable original Le Stylo paintings had mysteriously started appearing on the doorsteps of charities all over Paris with signed cards reading: LE STYLO IS NOT A THIEF.

Chief Olaf was a lot more willing to give us the inside scoop after our run-in with Chief Inspector Devereux that morning. He was still bristling over Devereux's insult, and just the mention of the inspector's name was enough to make him turn red.

"The Paris police have tails on a few suspects, and word is it couldn't have been Cyril Brune who delivered the paintings," he clued us in. "They've had eyes on him all day. He went to that gallery where they're showing Le Stylo's work earlier this afternoon and has been on his houseboat since. The packages were delivered after he got home."

"Houseboat?" I asked. I'd been about to tell Chief Olaf that we'd had a chance meeting of our own with Cyril at the gallery, but the mention of a houseboat totally got me sidetracked.

"He's got a place outside Paris too, but apparently that's where he stays when he's in the city," the chief explained. "Got it docked on the Seine under the Pont Alexandre III not far from here. Everybody says it's a real beaut."

A few other detectives joined in the conversation, and they were all trading rumors about Cyril when Inspector Devereux strode through the lobby like he owned the place. He sniffed in our direction as he walked past on the way to the manager's office, and I could see Chief Olaf clench his hands into fists. Even his fingers were turning red.

But Chief Olaf's skin wasn't the only flash of red that caught my eye. A beautiful red vintage Rolls-Royce limousine had pulled up in front of the hotel. The doorman went to talk to the chauffeur and then walked purposefully back through the lobby.

Devereux strutted over to greet him, apparently assuming that whatever important person had pulled up in the Rolls must be there for him, but the doorman walked right by him without a glance. We were just as surprised as everyone else when he approached and bowed to Joe and me instead.

"Pardon, messieurs," he said. "A car has arrived to escort the Hardy boys to Monsieur Brune's château."

PARTY CRASHERS

8

JOE

S
O THAT LITTLE GET-TOGETHER AT Cyril's place he invited us to? Well, the "get-together" was an extravagant art-world party, and his "place" was a castle! Literally a castle!

Cyril's château (that's French for "castle") was on a massive estate on the outskirts of Paris, and just about every inch of it was filled with French art. There was everything from pieces by lesser-known artists like Cosmonaute to huge pieces by Le Stylo and old master-works that looked like they should be in the Louvre. A real-life Vincent van Gogh painting of a human skull hung right next to a Georges St. Denis photograph showing a sign for Paris's famous catacombs—the ancient tunnels under the city where they kept the bones of millions of dead

Parisians—only Ratatouille had altered the sign so it read LES RATACOMBES instead of LES CATACOMBES. A cartoon rat skull in a red beret had been stenciled beside it.

There was an eclectic mix of people to match the artwork. Bohemian artist types mingled with upper-crust collectors, while waitstaff in tuxedos served everyone fancy hors d'oeuvres. There were some familiar faces there as well. Ginormo Luc was stuffing his face at the buffet table, while Simone Lachance was huddled in a corner with the short redheaded guy we'd heard criticizing Le Stylo at her gallery. He had the same camera around his neck and was gesturing wildly with his hands. We were too far away to hear anything, but from the looks of it, they were arguing.

"I wonder what that's all about," I said, pointing the conversation out to Frank.

"I'd say we should sneak closer and get a listen, but I think an old friend of ours might object," he cautioned.

I followed his eyes back to the buffet table, where Luc was now mad-dogging us over a half-eaten mutton chop. From the looks of him, he would have been happy to chomp down on us instead.

I quickly turned away and took in the rest of the crowd. "Recognize anyone else?"

"Nope," Frank replied. "Not even Cyril."

Frank was right: our host was nowhere to be seen. I looked down one of the long hallways branching off the main hall where everyone seemed to be congregating.

"Up for a self-guided tour?" I asked.

"I've always wanted to explore a European castle." Frank smiled. "And I don't see any 'Do Not Enter' signs."

"Not that that's ever stopped us before," I reminded him. "Lead the way, bro."

The corridor was lined with old paintings and statues on pedestals, and it seemed to go on forever. Just when I started to think maybe it actually did, a smaller hallway veered off to the left, and this one had a door at the end of it.

Giving a glance behind us to make sure we were alone, Frank headed right for it. After listening for a second to see if he could hear anything on the other side, he slowly turned the knob and cracked the door.

"Forget the Louvre," I gasped. "This is my kind of treasure."

We were staring into a garage the size of an airplane hangar, filled with some of the coolest vehicles I had ever seen in person. The garage wasn't just the size of an airplane hangar, though: it actually had an airplane in it. As well as a helicopter and a superexpensive assortment of gliders, race cars, motorcycles, off-road vehicles, and classic cars.

I eagerly followed Frank inside.

"Wow, it must be nice to be super rich," he observed, looking from the gleaming vehicles to the framed photographs on the wall of Cyril on adventures all around the world. Hang gliding over the Grand Canyon, free-climbing a rock face in the Andes, BASE jumping from a skyscraper in Dubai, diving with great white sharks.

"That was in the Neptune Islands off the coast of Australia," a smooth voice said from behind us.

We nearly jumped. Cyril had managed to sneak up behind us again!

"They wanted me to stay in the cage, but anyone can do that," he continued. "Great whites aren't the villains everyone makes them out to be. It was a powerful experience. And frightening."

I could see Frank shudder. We were both big on shark conservation, but we'd had underwater run-ins with our finned friends on a previous case, and I don't think either of us wanted to repeat the experience.

"We didn't know anyone at the party and thought it would be okay if we looked around," Frank said, trying to hide the fact that we'd been snooping. "Your house is amazing!"

Cyril laughed. "Well, I know all the people at the party, and I don't blame you for wanting to get away from them. I was doing the same thing. Everyone expects me to throw these lavish get-togethers, but to be honest, most of the people here bore me." He clapped us both on the shoulder. "Present company excluded."

Cyril caught me eyeing a superslick black dune buggy and grinned like a big kid. "Do you like my toys?"

"I like your definition of toy," I said.

"Would you like to take it for a spin?" he asked, a gleam in his eye as he walked over to the dune buggy and hit a concealed switch on the dash, releasing a hidden compartment with a key.

"For real?" Frank asked for both of us, since I was too excited to do anything except stand there with my mouth open.

"Unless you'd rather stand around making small talk with a bunch of boring art snobs," he said.

"Count me in!" I finally blurted. "For the driving part, I mean. Not the small talk part."

The little dune buggy was one of the coolest cars I'd ever seen. It basically looked like a mini Batmobile! It was about the size of Inspector Devereux's funky little two-seat European car, but that's where the similarity stopped. The buggy was elevated off the ground on big, fat off-road wheels that extended away from the body, giving it the appearance of a beast about to pounce. The whole thing was painted black, and every piece of metal was cut at sharp, aerodynamic angles. It even had a large, mean-looking propeller on the back like on an airboat. The whole thing was so sleek it could probably pass for a normal car as it zoomed down the street. But a close inspection made you think you were looking at something from the future.

"I bet this thing is fast!" I gushed.

"It's a Sky Ranger prototype," Cyril said as the engine roared to life. The name Sky Ranger rang a bell, like maybe I'd read about it on one of the auto or tech blogs I follow, but I couldn't quite place it.

"Totally street legal, with a max speed of a hundred eighty-five kilometers per hour on the ground," he continued.

"That's a hundred fifteen miles per hour!" Frank exclaimed.

By "on the ground," I figured Cyril meant a French way of saying maybe the road versus the racetrack. I was about to ask when I was interrupted by a high-pitched whining noise coming from somewhere down the road. It was a different tone from the one we had in America, but the sound was still unmistakable. Sirens.

Cyril closed his eyes, his smile vanishing as the sirens grew louder and flashing blue lights appeared through the garage's huge glass door. There was a procession of five police cars led by Inspector Devereux's funny-looking little French auto.

Cyril turned the Sky Ranger's engine off. "I suspect we'll have to save our ride for another time."

He walked over to the wall, hit the button to open the garage door, and stepped out confidently to meet the police. Guests were already pouring out of the house to see what was going on.

"*Bonsoir, Inspecteur,*" he greeted Devereux in French, then turned to the man who stepped out of the passenger seat beside him. "Monsieur."

"Inspector Livingston of Interpol's art crimes division," the man announced with a British accent. Interpol was Europe's international police force. Devereux had called in the big guns.

"I did not see your names on the guest list," Cyril said, switching to English. "But there is, of course, plenty of food for you and your officers if you are hungry."

"We have uncovered evidence incriminating you in this morning's theft." Devereux made sure to shout loud enough for everyone within earshot to hear. "We need you to come down to the station immediately."

"Can it wait until tomorrow? As you can see, I am entertaining at the moment." Cyril gestured to the gawking crowd. It looked like the whole party had come out to watch the spectacle.

"Justice does not wait for a rich man's parties," Devereux sneered.

"Am I under arrest, then?" Cyril asked calmly.

Devereux bristled.

"Not formally, sir," Inspector Livingston said respectfully.

"Yet," Devereux interjected. "But we can get a warrant easily enough if you refuse to cooperate."

Devereux nodded to one of the uniformed officers, who opened the back of his police car for Cyril to get in. Cyril didn't budge.

"I am always happy to cooperate with the police, Inspector," Cyril said smiling as if he weren't the least bit flustered. "But, seeing as I am still a free man, I think I'd prefer to drive myself . . . that is, if it's okay with you, of course."

"That should be fine, sir," Livingston agreed, as Devereux stood there stewing.

Cyril turned and called out to his guests as he walked back into the garage. "My apologies. I must leave early, but please feel free to stay and enjoy the refreshments in my absence."

Cyril put his hand on the Sky Ranger's roof and turned back to Devereux. "Do try to keep up, Inspector."

He hopped in without waiting for a reply, gunned the engine, and peeled out in a black buggy blur, leaving Devereux behind coughing up a cloud of dust.

FAMOUS LAST WORDS

9

FRANK

"HAND OVER YOUR PHONES," CHIEF Olaf barked as we walked back into the hotel later that night.

"*Bonsoir* to you, too, Chief," Joe said cheerily.

"Give 'em here," he demanded. "I don't want you boys mixed up with this Cyril Brune character until this Le Stylo business is sorted."

"What's Cyril Brune have to do with our phones?" I asked.

"Your father's flight isn't getting in until tomorrow at the earliest, and he'd never forgive me if I let you boys get arrested . . . or worse. So I'm going to install a GPS tracking app on your phones so I know where you are at all times." He held out his hand.

"You want us to let you spy on us?!" Joe asked, looking as flabbergasted as I felt. This was a new low, treating us like little kids.

"You're still minors and your father left you in my care, so unless you want to spend the rest of your vacation in your rooms . . ." He looked down at his open cell phone–less palms.

We both groaned. Then we gave him our phones.

"Can you at least tell us what happened?" Joe asked. "Is Cyril under arrest?"

The chief sighed, but he must have felt bad about installing spyware on our phones, because he answered, "They had to let him go."

Joe and I both smiled. Staying objective is critical to being a good detective, but it was hard not to like Cyril, and I was really hoping he wasn't our crook.

"But that doesn't mean he's innocent," Chief Olaf reminded us. "It just means they didn't have enough to charge him. But he visited the *Mona Lisa* exhibit yesterday, and they think he's the one who planted the projector. There were too many people and the camera angle was wrong to catch him doing it, but it sure looks suspicious."

The chief was right: it didn't prove anything, but it didn't look good, either. He saw our expressions sink and grumbled something to himself before continuing.

"If it makes you feel any better, your friend had a plausible excuse for being there. He's on some big art conservancy board and goes to the Louvre once a week, at least, so him visiting the *Mona Lisa* isn't all that unusual."

"I don't know how the law works over here, but all this sounds pretty circumstantial," I said, perking up. "It strengthens the case against him as a suspect, sure, but it doesn't prove anything."

"And the *Mona Lisa* gets, like, a hundred thousand visitors a day, right?" Joe added. "That's a lot of other people who could have planted the projector too."

"Which is exactly why they had to let him go. Word is Devereux was so mad he nearly threw a temper tantrum." The chief grinned. "They say he's been trying to catch Le Stylo for years and hates being shown up."

The image of Chief Inspector Devereux throwing a hissy fit made my brother and me grin as well.

"Devereux has a stakeout watching Cyril's houseboat, but apparently the only place he's gone since leaving the station is straight to sleep," Chief Olaf continued before adding, "Which is exactly what you boys need to do."

"Aw, Chief," Joe whined.

"Will you at least call our room to tell us if there are any new developments?" I pleaded.

The chief sighed again. "Some of the IPAD guys are pretty tied into the department here, so if he goes anywhere, we'll all hear about it. Now, it's been a long day, and it's time for all of us to turn in."

We took back our bugged phones and trudged to the

room. Not like either of us were about to get any sleep after the day we'd had. The jet lag had our internal clocks all wonky and the case had our minds wired.

"I sure would like to get a look at that houseboat," I sighed, lying in my twin bed staring at the ceiling.

"I was hoping you would say that," Joe said, hopping out of bed and laying his phone on the table. "And as long as we leave our phones in the room, the chief won't know the difference."

I grinned. "He's got enough on his mind. We wouldn't want him to worry."

A twenty-minute midnight stroll along the Seine later and we were standing on the Pont Alexandre III, one of the most famous bridges in all of Paris. Docked on the Left Bank beneath the ornate lanterns and statues of golden-winged horses was Cyril's houseboat—a beautiful fifty-foot, two-story dark wood floating home.

"Cyril really does have the best toys." Joe sighed longingly as he pulled out a pair of binoculars from his bag.

I nodded. "Looks like the lights are out on this one, though."

"Yeah, not much to see as far as the case goes. The only thing I can tell is that Inspector Devereux's detectives have weak stakeout skills." Joe handed me the binoculars and pointed to a car parked on the other side of the bridge right beneath a streetlight. It was easy to see two policemen inside guzzling coffee and chowing down on pastries.

"I guess some things really are the same in every country," he quipped.

"If Cyril is Le Stylo, he'd be way too smart to do anything suspicious with them right there," I noted. Watching the houseboat sway gently in the calm Seine waters was finally making me sleepy. "Maybe we should call it a night." I handed him the binoculars back.

Joe yawned in agreement and looked around at the scene one last time.

We had just started to turn back when . . .

"Hey, what's that?" Joe pointed to a ring of bubbles floating to the surface by the houseboat.

"Huh, *les poissons*, maybe?" I suggested. That's French for "fish."

"Then what's that?" Joe pointed to the houseboat's roof . . . where a small black drone suddenly whirred into the air and took off down the Seine, chasing after the bubbles!

"I don't know how you say it in French, but that's a spy drone!" I said as we both started running along the Left Bank in pursuit of the tiny helicopter with its four swirling rotors.

The French cops in the car across the street were too occupied with their *pâtisseries* to notice, so it was up to us. Only the drone was moving way faster than we could keep up with. At least not on foot.

Which is why it's a good thing Cyril left his supersweet

Sky Ranger buggy parked a block down the street. I saw it before Joe did and started to slow down.

"Hey, the drone's going to get away . . . ," Joe started to complain until he saw the buggy for himself. "Ohhhh."

A big grin spread across his face. "Cyril did offer to let us take it for a spin."

"And we do know where the key is," I added.

We both hopped in without a second thought, Joe in the driver's seat and me riding shotgun. Joe popped open the secret compartment with the key, cranked the engine, and . . .

"Follow that drone!" I shouted.

And we were off!

"This is awesome!" Joe hollered, the wind whipping in our faces as we zipped down the street hugging the Left Bank.

Normally I'm a little more cautious than my brother about things like driving "borrowed" cars in a foreign country without a license, but . . .

"Whoo-hoo!" I shouted.

. . . this was just way too much fun!

The drone was flying right over the river, so it was easy to follow. I couldn't help taking my eyes off it to check out the buggy's sleek dashboard. It was a lot more streamlined than a normal car, with a handful of cool James Bond spy-car-looking buttons. It was the big red one right in the middle of the console that caught my eye.

My finger was in motion before I could stop myself, my

mouth uttering the five famous last words you never want to hear while racing around in a stolen super-high-tech Batmobile-looking prototype car: "What does this button do?"

There was a clicking noise followed by a whooshing noise, and I knew it was a mistake as soon as I said it.

"Maybe you shouldn't . . . ," Joe began to protest, but it was already too late. The button had been pressed—the button that releases the collapsible paraglider wing we didn't know was hidden in the back of the buggy!

"Oops," I squeaked, clutching my seat as the little car lurched off the ground and up into the sky.

"I don't want to find out how fast it goes in the air," Frank shrieked. "But I guess we know why they call it a Sky Ranger!"

That's when it clicked. "I knew I'd heard the name Sky Ranger before!" I called over the whoosh of the air and the whir of the rear propeller. "It's one of the first flying cars! I saw rumors about it on online last year. People are paying a hundred grand just to get on a list to buy one, but it's just a prototype. It hasn't even gone into production yet."

"Cyril is full of surprises," Frank croaked. "A flying car would definitely help explain how Le Stylo pulled off some of his other impossible stunts."

"I bet we're the first teenagers in the world to fly a car over Paris," I shouted, suddenly filled with excitement.

"I'd rather be the first teenagers to safely land a car in Paris," Frank moaned.

My excitement turned back to fear pretty quickly when I looked down. We were still only a few yards off the ground, but the car was steadily gaining altitude, and nothing I did seemed to stop it.

I also saw something else when I looked down—the thing the drone had been chasing. The drone had slowed to a halt and was hovering in the shadows over the Right Bank . . . where a small one-man submersible scooter rose to the surface!

"Look down, bro!" I shouted to Frank.

"I don't want to!" he shouted back.

"Trust me," I said as the person riding the underwater

THE FLYING DETECTIVES

10

JOE

I WATCHED IN THE REARVIEW MIRROR AS THE forty-foot-wide parachute unfurled from the back of the buggy and caught air, rising over us like a fabric wing on strings. I glanced down to see the wheels folding into the car. Before I could figure out how to stop it, we were airborne. Our midnight ride had turned into midnight flight!

"I'm usually the one doing boneheaded things like pressing the red button," I yelled, frantically trying to figure the controls as the car soared into the sky over the Seine.

"I know," Frank whimpered. "I'm sorry. It was just so r

"Cyril saying the Sky Ranger could do a hundred fif miles per hour on the ground suddenly makes a lot sense," I reflected.

scooter took off their scuba mask. Even from up here, I could tell it was . . .

"Cyril!" Frank exclaimed. "Could he really be Le Stylo?"

"I've seen submersibles like that online," I said. "They're great for shallow dives, and they let a diver cover a lot of ground quickly. He must have launched it from a secret portal under the houseboat."

"If Cyril is Le Stylo, that would explain how he snuck away from the houseboat to deliver all those paintings to the charities yesterday without the police seeing him leave," Frank observed.

Cyril stashed his scuba gear and was climbing up to the street, the spy drone trailing unnoticed at a safe distance, when I turned my full attention back to the Sky Ranger's controls. The internal combustion engine had shut down when the buggy took off, and it was quiet enough that we might have been able to keep following Cyril from the sky, if:

(a) we weren't headed in the wrong direction, and . . .

(b) I knew how to drive a flying car!

"Can you swing around to follow him?" Frank asked.

"No!" I shouted.

"Do I want to know why not?" Frank asked more meekly.

"No!"

"You don't have control over this thing, do you?"

"No!"

"Um, is that the Eiffel Tower we're headed for?"

"Yes!"

UFO: UNCONTROLLABLE

FLYING OBJECT

11

FRANK

THE LE STYLO CASE HADN'T JUST taken a twist, it had taken a dive and a lift-off as well. Normally my mind would be racing to put the pieces together, but we had bigger things to worry about than whether Cyril was Le Stylo or who knew enough to follow him with a drone. Nine hundred eighty-four feet bigger!

The flying car soared higher and the Eiffel Tower loomed closer, its impossibly tall steel legs rising into a sky-high spear of death ready to pulverize us if Joe didn't figure out how to steer this thing quick. I'd wanted to see the Eiffel Tower while we were in Paris, but . . .

"This wasn't the kind of sightseeing I had in mind!" I screamed. "Do something!"

"I'm trying!" Joe screamed back, yanking hard on the wheel and working the pedals like mad.

We were so close I could see the pins holding the beams together. And then the weld marks. And then . . . we were out of time. The buggy was moving too fast. I shut my eyes, unable to watch the moment of our—

"Yes!" Joe shouted.

I felt the car jerk hard to the left and opened my eyes in time to see the tower's steel beams whoosh past close enough to touch.

"Way to go, Joe!" I cheered as the buggy zipped around the Eiffel Tower with Joe now firmly in control.

"Dude, did you ever doubt me?" he asked.

"Yes," I said, barely able to hear my voice over my own thumping heart. "Absolutely."

"Me too," he said with a grin. "But now that I have the hang of it, this is amazing!"

I looked down. The view was beyond amazing. All of Paris spread out below us in a sea of lights. You could see everything at once. The Seine aglow in the reflection of the streetlamps as it snaked through the city. The Louvre pyramid and all the other famous landmarks shining with light. There was one thing we couldn't see, though.

"There's no way we're finding Cyril or that drone now," I said.

"Well, we definitely learned one thing tonight . . . ," Joe began.

"Don't drive a flying car into one of the most famous landmarks in the world?" I asked.

"That too," he agreed. "But with his flying Batmobile buggy and secret alter ego, Cyril is practically a French Bruce Wayne."

"Either he's Le Stylo, or he's going to an insane amount of trouble to defend whoever is," I asserted.

"Either way, I'm starting to think what Cyril insinuated at the gallery could be true," Joe shared. "Maybe Le Stylo didn't pull the *Mona Lisa* stunt and the Napoléon pen heist after all."

"Do you think it's whoever was piloting that drone?" I asked. "It sure didn't seem like Cyril knew it was following him."

"Whoever was behind that drone knew enough about Cyril's secrets to spy on the houseboat and wait for the submersible to launch," Joe went on, keeping the theory cranking. "Which means if Cyril really is Le Stylo, then the spy also knows enough about his methods to convincingly make the Louvre hoax look like Le Stylo's handiwork."

"And frame him like a painting," I added.

I looked back down at Paris glowing beneath us. Our villain was down there somewhere.

"Any chance that Cyril is Le Stylo and *did* do it?" I theorized. "He could have given away all those paintings as a publicity stunt to save his image and still get away with it."

"But why?" Joe wanted to know. "What would he have to gain by stealing Plouffe's pen? We know he doesn't need the money, not when he turned right around and gave away over a million dollars' worth of his own paintings the next day."

"Speaking of Plouffe, if Simone Lachance is right about him profiting off the theft through his insurance policy, then that gives him a motive too," I said, trying on a new theory. "If he stole the pen from himself, he'd make back more than he spent to buy it and also get to keep it for free."

"He really did seem distraught, though. He'd have to be a really good actor," Joe pointed out. "And he couldn't have stolen it by himself, because he was with us when the thief took the safe. So he'd have to have an accomplice."

"If he did, we can be pretty certain it wasn't Simone. If she was his partner, she wouldn't have drawn attention to him by talking about his insurance policy," I said, chipping away at the proposition of a Plouffe conspiracy. "He also didn't know anyone was listening when we overheard him on the phone asking for her help finding it. He wouldn't have been crying about his stolen treasure to the person who helped him steal it."

"What about Ginormo Luc?" Joe shuddered.

"As much as I dislike the guy, what's his motive?" I asked. "Even if he had one, he's got to be three hundred pounds at least. Whoever scaled the pyramid in that mirrored suit would have to have weighed a lot less."

"Yeah, and the police definitely would have noticed him on the security cameras if he visited the *Mona Lisa* when the projector was planted," Joe agreed.

"Maybe Devereux had something to do with it." I tossed out the name of our other least favorite person in France. "I don't like to think about the implications of a police officer betraying his oath like that, but he has a motive. Chief Olaf said he's been after Le Stylo for years. Showing up the police is Le Stylo's specialty, and Devereux hates getting shown up."

"But if he was the one behind the drone, that would mean he already knew enough about Cyril to bust him. Why go to all this other trouble?" Joe wondered.

"Unless he knew because he'd been spying illegally and needed legally admissible evidence to nail Cyril without nailing himself as a crooked cop in the process," I suggested.

"Hmm. I don't know, bro, seems a little thin," Joe said, steering the Sky Ranger back to Cyril's houseboat.

I sighed. We were running out of suspects and I was grasping at straws.

"Do we know anything about that redheaded guy with the camera we saw arguing with Simone at Cyril's party?" I asked. "They both had bones to pick with Le Stylo. I wonder what bones they had with each other. And all three of them seem to know one another."

"Yeah, but Cyril is a huge collector. He and Simone probably know a ton of the same art-world people," Joe said, casting doubt on another of my theories. "We'd need to know more about him to see if there was a connection worth exploring. And all those other artists we heard talking around the Georges St. Denis exhibit seemed pretty sour about Le Stylo's success too."

"Could it be another street artist, then?" I asked. "You said a lot of street artists have rivalries with one another, like how Cosmonaute and Ratatouille try to outdo each other with their imitations of famous artwork like Monet or the *Mona Lisa.*"

Joe thought about it for a moment. "I don't know. Le Stylo is on another level from those other guys, and I've never seen him bother with rivalries. Cosmonaute has spoofed Le Stylo with tile mosaics, and Ratatouille has burned Le Stylo pieces before—"burning" is when one street artist paints over another artist's work. There's one where he stenciled over Le Stylo's soldiers carrying fountain pens to change the pens into baguettes and gave the soldiers red berets, whiskers, and rat tails. But it's a pretty big leap from painting over someone's work to pulling one of the most elaborate stunts in art history."

"Good point," I conceded. "Well, tomorrow I say we dig up some more info on the redhead with the camera and those other artists from the gallery. And I think we should have another chat with Monsieur Plouffe to see if there's anything to the insurance scam theory."

Joe nodded, his focus on directing the Sky Ranger back toward the houseboat.

"I'm fresh out of ideas. You have any theories you want to share about whodunit instead of just shooting down mine?" I quipped.

Joe shook his head. "But I bet Cyril does."

"I say we ask him."

"Good plan," Joe said. "Just as soon as I figure out how to land a flying car."

"Ughh . . . ," I moaned, my head swirling with vertigo as I looked down. Staying in the air was stressful enough; I hadn't thought about landing!

"Paris seems to be full of narrow, twisty old streets," Joe observed. "They don't exactly make ideal runways."

Fighting back my dizziness, I took in the city below. A glowing, super-wide thoroughfare north of where Cyril had emerged from the Seine grabbed my attention.

"But that might." Joe pointed to the Champs-Élysées—Paris's most famous street, with ten beautiful lanes and not that much traffic late at night.

"Absolutely not!" I yelled. "We're just going to have to risk using one of the side streets. We can't land this thing on one of the most famous landmarks in Paris and not get caught. And I have no idea how we would talk our way out of this one."

I eyed the ornate 164-foot-tall, 148-foot-wide stone arch in the middle of an immense traffic circle, where the Champs-Élysées intersected with ten other roads. The Arc de Triomphe might not have been as tall as the Eiffel Tower, but it was still breathtaking, even from this high up.

"Okay, okay. I think I can manage," Joe said, maneuvering the little car over the traffic. "But first, let's check another landmark off your sightseeing list!"

The Arc de Triomphe sped closer, but Joe maintained control. Just as we zoomed past it, Le Stylo's name appeared projected in huge letters on the front of the arch. More words followed, spreading across the arch as if by magic: LE STYLO N'EST PAS UN VOLEUR.

"Le Stylo isn't a thief," I translated.

I looked back as a second sentence appeared projected in English on the other side: IMITATION IS THE SINCEREST FORM OF FRAMING ME.

Joe read the message through the rearview mirror.

"Well, now I guess we know what Cyril's been up to since we saw him climb out of the river."

PEN PALS 12

JOE

WE'D LEARNED A COUPLE OF NIFTY new details about the case on our surprise flight over Paris. Cyril was either Le Stylo or he was posing as him to advertise the artist's innocence. And he had come to the same conclusion that we had: Le Stylo was probably being framed for the theft of Plouffe's precious pen.

Luckily, we were able to find and land on a deserted side street. It may not have been an expert landing, but I think I did pretty well, considering I had no idea what I was doing. And I'm almost positive no one saw us land. I made Frank sit on his hands so he wasn't tempted to push any more buttons, and drove as carefully as possible back to the Pont Alexander III, where I parked the flying buggy right where we'd found it.

"The lights are still out on the houseboat," Frank observed. "No way to tell if Cyril has snuck back on board yet."

"And with the cops still watching, we can't just go up and knock on his door," I said, eyeing the unmarked cop car still parked on the corner.

Frank smiled as he watched me pop Sky Ranger's key back into the secret compartment. "We could always leave him a note somewhere the police won't know to look."

"Good call," I said, pulling out the small pocket notebook I carry with me to log case notes.

We forgot our swim trunks, so we took you up on your offer to go for a spin. The ride was illuminating, I scribbled, tipping him off that we were onto his midnight dive to project Le Stylo's message across the Arc de Triomphe. *Leave the critics behind and give a couple of street art fans a private art history lesson . . . before they have to take their review public. Café Aventure @ 10.*

I folded the note and tucked it inside the hidden compartment along with the key.

"Do you think he'll show?" Frank asked.

"Well, we know he won't have a problem ditching the stakeout detail," I replied. "And he probably knows he'll get a fairer shake from us than Devereux."

We walked back to the hotel and caught a few hours of shut-eye before our maybe-rendezvous. When we made it down to the lobby the next morning, all the IPAD attendees were buzzing, and this time it wasn't about Le Stylo.

"There is no such thing as UFOs!" a woman with a Spanish accent declared.

"At least fifty people from all over Paris called the police last night to report seeing it buzz by the Eiffel Tower and head for the Arc de Triomphe," countered our English friend Stucky. "I'm not saying it was aliens, but it was unidentified, it was flying, and it was an object. That makes it a UFO!"

"Oops," uttered Frank as we exchanged a guilty look. It looked like our late night flight in Cyril's flying dune buggy had attracted some unwanted attention . . . from half of Paris!

"If I didn't know better, I'd say this alien business had something to do with you," Chief Olaf prodded before we could slip by unnoticed.

"Consorting with aliens?" I asked in my best shocked voice. "We've had secret sources on cases before, but as far as I know, they've all been from this galaxy."

"I wouldn't put it past you after some of the crazy things you boys have gotten involved in back in Bayport," he shot back.

The chief kind of had a point—we'd had run-ins on recent cases with everything from sharks to cursed ancient underground cults to crazy mountain men.

"We couldn't have been the aliens," Frank added a little too defensively. "We were in bed all night."

Chief Olaf eyed us suspiciously—but thankfully, the chief eyeing us suspiciously was a pretty much daily thing.

"I guess we'll be in the chief's neighborhood after all. I hope he won't be offended if we don't call him."

A half-hour Métro ride later and we were standing in front of a nondescript gated apartment building on a nondescript street without another person in sight.

"I don't see any green windmills," I quipped.

"I don't see where we're supposed to go," countered Frank. "There are probably fifty different apartment units at this address and no call box with the people's names."

I took in the rest of the sad little street. It wasn't nearly as nice or bustling as any of the other Paris neighborhoods we'd seen so far. The only things there besides neglected-looking apartments were a few town houses with boarded-up storefronts that looked like they'd been closed for years. The one across the street had been a butcher, and the one next to number 31 had a faded sign that said PAPETERIE, with pictures of fancy paper, pens, and notebooks.

"An out-of-business butcher and a stationery store," Frank said, reading the signs and tugging uselessly on the locked stationery store door. "Not that that does us any good."

And that's when it clicked.

"A stationery store! Where they sold pens! I bet this place is a front for . . ."

And then something else clicked.

The door.

"Le Stylo," Frank finished my sentence.

He looked around to make sure the street was still empty and tried the door again. This time it opened. Someone had buzzed us in.

We stepped cautiously inside the empty shop, stepping over the discarded boxes littering the dusty floor. The door clicked locked behind us.

"I hope this isn't a bad idea," I whispered, checking my pocket to make sure my cell phone was still safely inside. The idea of the chief being able to track our location suddenly seemed a lot less annoying now that we were locked inside a criminal's secret hideout.

A disembodied voice broke the silence through the old intercom mounted on the wall above the broken cash register.

"Third floor," Cyril said calmly. "The stairs are to your right."

We emerged from the stairwell into a large, well-decorated office that looked totally out of place with the neglected building and vacant stationery store.

"I thought my private office might be a quieter place to chat," Cyril said from behind the desk.

"I take it the police don't have any idea you're here," I prompted, wondering just how safe we were if Cyril decided to turn on us. You never knew what a cornered criminal would do, even a nice one.

"The police are intently watching the office building across town where I parked my car two hours ago," he confirmed. "Paris is full of wonderful old tunnels. It's easy to get from one place to another unseen if you know where you're going."

"Like the manager's office at our hotel," Frank suggested.

Cyril frowned. "I found out that was there when the news of the theft of Napoléon's pen broke, just like the rest of Paris."

"Do you have an alibi?" Frank pressed him.

"No, and that should be proof enough. Had it been me, I certainly would." He gestured to his secret office. "You should know by now that I'm quite skilled at accounting for my time whenever I'm somewhere I'm not supposed to be. You'll also find I have rock-solid alibis for every other stunt Le Stylo has ever pulled. It's what's given Devereux such fits. If I'm Le Stylo, as you suggest—not that I am, of course, but just supposing—then why would I slip up this once?"

He had a point. I'd never met someone so good at being in two places at the same time. He'd been sneaking all over Paris for the past two days while the police twiddled their thumbs watching empty houseboats and office buildings.

"Being good at deceiving the police is an odd way of trying to prove your innocence," Frank baited him. "And Le Stylo has been provoking the authorities for years."

"Theft goes against everything I stand for!" he shouted. Frank had pushed a button. It was the first time we'd seen Cyril lose his cool.

"And by you, you mean Le Stylo?" I nudged.

"I . . ." He stopped and took a deep breath to compose

himself. "You boys are much better detectives than my dear friend Inspector Devereux."

Cyril might have been too clever to come right out and say it, but it was as good as a confession.

He held up the note we'd left for him in the Sky Ranger. "You are a step ahead of me, and a mile ahead of the police."

"We usually are," I told him. "Some things are pretty much the same in any country."

"Which is why I want your help finding out who framed me," Cyril declared.

"Why should we trust you?" Frank asked.

"For the same reason I'm trusting you," he answered. "Because I believe you are decent young men who care about doing the right thing. Otherwise you'd be at the police station ratting me out to Devereux instead of here, giving me a chance to explain."

Frank and I exchanged a look. I could tell he was thinking the same thing I was. Our dad had a saying: *Never trust a suspect. Trust your instincts.* And my instincts were saying . . .

"We'll see."

Cyril nodded. "Thank you. That will have to be good enough."

"So you're saying you didn't pull off the *Mona Lisa* prank either?" I queried.

"That part of it I almost wish I had. It was brilliant. And it mimicked Le Stylo precisely. It's as if someone's been studying my every move," he mused.

"Because they have," I told him.

"Apparently we're not the only ones a step ahead of you," Frank said. "Someone else followed you last night as well. They had a drone camped out on top of the houseboat, waiting for you to launch that slick submersible scooter of yours. It must have been a really good one too, since it was able to follow you all over the city."

Cyril jerked back like he'd been slapped. "But who would do that?!"

"We were kind of hoping you could tell us that," Frank said.

"I thought the thief was merely a copycat," Cyril said in disbelief. "I am very careful to keep my secrets to myself and have been since the beginning."

"In our line of work, you learn that there are no safe secrets when it comes to breaking the law," Frank said.

Cyril's cool facade had crumbled. He slumped in his seat and looked nervously around the office like the bad guy might be hiding behind the blinds at that very moment.

"Can you think of anyone?" Frank persisted. "What about Simone Lachance? She handles both Le Stylo the artist and Cyril the art buyer."

"I was especially careful with Simone," he said. "There's no way she could have found out unless someone else told her."

"Maybe Mr. Nib is the weak link," I suggested.

He avoided answering the question directly. "I have a

butler I trust implicitly. Even if I didn't, his whereabouts are well accounted for."

"How about Plouffe? Simone hinted that he might have profited from the pen's theft," Frank said, running through our list of suspects.

Cyril shook his head no. "I've never even met the man. His art circle and mine rarely overlap."

"And Devereux?" I asked, throwing him our wildest theory. "Sounds like you've been making a fool out of him for years. Getting in on the frame might be a good way for him to turn the tables."

"Devereux is a pompous bore and a downright mediocre detective, but he has never struck me as dishonest," Cyril stated.

"And you're sure none of your friends or family know?" I asked, looking around at some of the photos decorating his office. He sure led a cool life. Black-tie parties with beautiful women. Schmoozing with painters and sculptors in their studios. Captaining a yacht during a sailing regatta. Standing on top of Mount Everest posing with his climbing buddies.

"My parents died when I was young, and there's no other family I like enough to stay in touch with," he shared. "I am a very private person with many acquaintances and few real friends. I do not let anyone know more about me than I want them to know."

A flash of red in one of the pictures caught my eye. Cyril

was in a big art studio with a bunch of artists, only this one was different from the other pictures. For one, Cyril was a lot younger—in college from the looks of it—and he was surrounded by friends the same age, all of them paint-splattered and happy. And I recognized one of them. Or his hair, more precisely. I walked over to the wall to get a closer look.

Cyril had his arm around a short guy with bright red hair, a face like a rodent, and a camera around his neck. The same guy who had been talking trash about Le Stylo's work at Galerie Simone and arguing with Simone herself at Cyril's party. He looked so familiar, but I still couldn't put my finger on where else I'd seen him.

"Who's this guy with the red hair?" I pointed.

Cyril got up and stood beside me to look at the picture. "My old classmate Georges St. Denis. That was taken right before I got kicked out of art school."

"Georges St. Denis the photographer from Galerie Simone?" Frank clarified right away. That explained the connection between the redhead and Simone.

"Yes. I got him that show, in fact," Cyril revealed. "His career's been in need of a boost, and I always try to support my former art school colleagues. Not everyone's as lucky as I am to be able to fund their own artistic pursuits. I've purchased a number of his photographs as well. I just brought one back from the gallery to hang here, actually."

He gestured to a framed picture still wrapped in brown paper, leaning against one of the walls.

"You know he's not Le Stylo's biggest fan, right?" I asked, thinking about how bitter he'd sounded about the outlaw artist's success.

"Did you overhear one of his rants at the gallery?" Cyril chuckled. "I actually agree with some of it. I was honest with you when I said I wasn't sure what I thought of Le Stylo's work. I've never been very confident in my own skill as an artist; but I'd like to think the message and presentation make up for any shortcomings in talent."

"So you don't think Georges has an ax to grind?" Frank pressed further.

"Oh, Georges was always a sourpuss when it came to other artists' success, but I don't take it personally. It's not like he thinks he's criticizing me," he said confidently.

"But it's not like your cover is without cracks, right?" I asked. "I mean, the police suspect that you're Le Stylo. And so does the media. Maybe Georges agrees with them?"

"No, he would think that it's all rumors. As far as Georges or anyone else from art school knows, I never picked up a paintbrush again after getting kicked out of school my freshman year. Everyone assumed I was a spoiled rich kid who was more interested in having fun than hard work, so I let them. Truth was, my dreams were bigger than any of theirs, although not the kind I wanted to attract attention to myself for. I knew art school wasn't for me that first semester. We were all captivated by the street art scene back then—not that our teachers thought much of it. As soon as inspiration struck for my, shall we say, alter artistic ego, I decided to let my formal education be a short one and made a public show of my career as an artist burning out before it began."

"When in reality you were secretly creating your own mysterious street art superstar," I tacked on the part he hadn't mentioned.

Cyril just smiled.

I picked up the wrapped picture frame and peeled back the brown paper to reveal the Georges St. Denis photograph Cyril had just purchased. It was the same one that had first grabbed my attention at Galerie Simone.

Ratatouille looked back from the camera shop window through the lens of his own vintage camera as if the cartoon rat had taken the picture of himself in the window's reflection. I read the photograph's title, handwritten in French along the bottom border beside Georges St. Denis's signature.

"*Autoportrait*," I read aloud. "What does that mean?"

"Self-portrait, I think," Frank replied.

Cyril continued talking, unconcerned by the photograph. "There's never been the slightest hint that any of my class-mates suspected I was anything but what I seemed to be. And as generous as I've been supporting their careers, even on the off chance they had, why would any of them want to rat me out?"

"'Rat you out . . .'" I repeated Cyril's words quietly to myself as I stared at St. Denis's "self-portrait" of Ratatouille with a camera to his eye. And that's when the missing piece of cheese fell into place. "I know why Georges St. Denis looks so familiar!"

Frank and Cyril both looked at me as I looked from the photograph of Ratatouille's human-size rat in his trademark bright red beret to the college picture of Georges, short and mousy-looking with a head full of bright red hair.

"Georges St. Denis isn't mousy-looking; he's ratty-looking!" I shouted, unable to contain the excitement over my discovery.

Cyril just stared at me in confusion. "He always was a little ratty-looking. Some of our classmates used to tease him about it even. What of it?"

"Not just ratty-looking—he's downright Ratatouille-looking!" Frank blurted, catching on.

It wasn't the type of thing you'd automatically notice if you weren't looking for it, but now that I'd spotted it, the resemblance was unmistakable. The facial features were more exaggerated, of course, and the red hair had been replaced by a red beret, but . . .

"Either it's a huge coincidence or Ratatouille is a self-caricature," I declared.

Cyril still couldn't seem to wrap his mind around it. "But that would mean . . ."

He let the sentence trail off, so I filled in the rest for him.

"Georges *is* Ratatouille."

13

FRANK

"LE STYLO DOESN'T HAVE A COPYCAT," Joe said, holding the framed photograph of Ratatouille looking through the camera up for Cyril. "He has a copy-rat."

Cyril's unflappable Bruce Wayne meets James Bond mask flapped as he looked in stunned disbelief from the photo of Ratatouille to the college picture of Georges and back again.

"I don't think it's an accident that Ratatouille is Georges St. Denis's favorite photography subject," I said as it dawned on me how clever Georges had been. "Joe is right. That isn't just a photo of a stencil of Ratatouille taking a picture, it's a self-portrait of the photographer. He's hiding the clues right in his artwork."

"They're even the same height." Joe pointed to how much shorter he was than Cyril in their college picture. "Ratatouille may be a monster-size rat, but he's pretty short for a grown-up dude. Just like your friend Georges."

"It has to be a coincidence. There's no way it—it's—" Cyril stammered, struggling to accept the possibility that he wasn't the only street artist he knew with a shocking secret identity. "It's uncanny. How could I have missed it before? A good artist is supposed to have the eye of an observer."

"Kind of like being a good detective," I related. "A lot of time the truth is hidden right in front of you. You just have to figure out where to look."

"I've been so preoccupied protecting my own secrets, I never stopped to think other people I know might have secrets of their own as well. Could he really have been living a double life right in front of me this whole time?" From the tone of Cyril's voice, he already knew the answer.

"And if Georges was able to hide his alter ego from you . . . ," I began, giving Cyril a chance to connect the dots for himself.

"He could have hidden his knowledge of mine as well," he conceded.

Cyril picked up the photograph of Ratatouille. "He's been flaunting it right in my face. He's practically bragging about making a fool of me."

"I don't think that's all he's bragging about," Joe said, pulling out his phone. A second later he was on Instagram, typing the #ratatouille hashtag into the search bar to pull up pics of all the artist's latest pieces. "He's been flaunting it in everyone in Paris's face."

The first image that popped up was of Ratatouille's smirking face on the *Mona Lisa*, and I realized that Joe was dead-on. "It's like the self-portrait. All the Ratatouille street art we've seen tells a hidden story, only none of it seems suspicious on its own until you know to look for it and start adding up the pieces."

I looked at the post's date and location. "I don't think it's an accident that this one showed up right around the corner from the Louvre two days before the *Mona Lisa* hoax."

"There's also the one we saw this morning of him as the Sphinx on the bus stop across the street from the museum. It even incorporates the glass pyramid so it looks like part of the composition. It's like he's crowning himself king of the Louvre," Joe said, scrolling farther down the screen.

There was another new one we hadn't seen before of Ratatouille dressed like the famous fictional detective Sherlock Holmes, bending over with a magnifying glass to examine a rodent-size door by his feet, revealing a sign taped to his back that read KICK ME.

"That one's on the wall right behind our hotel, where all the detectives from around the world are staying for the IPAD convention!" I announced, recognizing the street name that the Instagram user who posted the pic had tagged as the location.

"He's been using his street art to boast about the crime he was planning—stealing Napoléon's pen," Joe stated confidently. "Scaling the pyramid at the Louvre, the vanishing *Mona Lisa* hoax, taunting the detectives staying right across the street to try and catch him. He's staking his claim to all of it through his art."

"Even the first one we saw when we arrived in Paris was of him stealing something," I said, thinking about the stencil of Ratatouille sneaking off into the sewer with a baguette. "He's advertising to the whole world that he's a thief."

"A rat burglar," Joe spat.

"Georges always did like to remind people he thought he was smarter than everyone else," Cyril seethed.

"It must have really irked him, then, knowing your work got all the acclaim while Ratatouille was still a small-time street artist," Joe speculated.

Cyril gave a bitter little laugh. "Georges has been going on for years about how simplistic and obvious he thought Le Stylo's artwork was, and I'd told him I thought the same of Ratatouille. I guess he got the last laugh."

"Not yet he hasn't," I reminded him, turning to Joe. "Can you map where all those pictures were taken?"

Joe found an Instagram account dedicated to Ratatouille's work and tapped the location icon that showed where all the pictures were taken around Paris. There were little image icons spread all over the city, but the majority of them were clustered in two places.

"The drone!" Joe shouted.

"It's seen us," I said, then grinned. Thanks to the pigeons, we'd seen it too. "Let's catch that flying rat!"

The drone zipped off over the rooftops, and we took off running down the street after it.

I called out to Joe as we ran. "As long as it doesn't duck down behind the buildings across the street, we should be able to . . . oops."

"There it goes," Joe grumbled as the drone did exactly what we didn't want it to. "Look! It's descending. Maybe if we cut across that alley we can still intercept it."

I followed Joe across the street and down the alley.

We ran around the bend and came to an abrupt stop. Not because of what we saw, but because of what we didn't. We could see clear down the rest of the alley all the way to the next street . . . except there was nothing there.

"Where could the drone have gone? We saw it descending down here."

Joe looked around, scratching his head.

We stepped over an old sewer grate and proceeded cautiously down the narrow alleyway. I noticed the grate was off to the side, leaving an opening into the sewer below.

"It couldn't have just vanished into thin air," Joe complained.

"That's it!" I said.

Joe looked at me like I was crazy. "I think this case is going to your head, bro."

"'Just vanished . . . ,'" I repeated, running back to the old sewer grate. "All of Ratatouille's work reveals secret clues about Georges, right? Think about what Rat-Man was doing in the first piece we saw by the bakery when we got to Paris."

"He vanished underground!" Joe put the pieces together. "Of course. Just like he got away when he stole the pen from the hotel."

"What better place to look for a rat than in a sewer? Give me a hand," I grunted, straining to lift off the grate. It came free a lot easier than I expected, though, and I almost fell on my rump.

"This must be one of his regular escape routes." Joe peered into the darkness below. "And this time there's no smoke bomb to hide his trail."

Joe switched on his phone's flashlight, illuminating a trail of wet sneaker prints scampering off through the damp tunnel at the bottom of a rusty old ladder.

I followed Joe down the ladder into the sewer. The trail of footprints didn't go far before dead-ending at a huge pile of rubble blocking the path beyond. Some of the rocks had been pulled out about halfway up to create a gap big enough for someone to crawl through.

"A lot of the old tunnels were sealed off by the city years ago because so many people kept getting lost or hurt," I whispered. "I bet this is one of them."

Joe took a deep breath as he stepped forward toward the gap in the wall. "Let's hope we don't get lost or hurt either."

I took a deep breath of my own and joined him. The gap led to a crawl space through the rubble that went on for a few yards. I couldn't see anything on the other side except total darkness.

"He's probably far enough ahead by now that we can't see whatever light he's using," Joe guessed. "Unless I'm wrong and he's waiting on the other side to ambush us."

I gulped. "Maybe we shouldn't . . ."

But the top half of Joe's body had already disappeared into the crawl space.

"Wait for me," I said, climbing in after him and hurrying to catch up. I didn't want to be in that crawl space any longer than I had to.

The "ceiling" was nothing but packed rubble, and I wasn't especially confident it wouldn't cave in on us. The crawl space was just big enough for me to squeeze alongside Joe, and I had to fight back claustrophobia as we crept the final few feet. I didn't think it could get any worse than being trapped inside. I was wrong.

Our flashlights finally pierced the darkness and I choked back a scream. Someone was waiting for us in the next tunnel after all, and it wasn't Georges St. Denis.

My eyes went wide—but not as wide as the thousand unseeing eye sockets gaping back at us.

CITY OF THE DEAD

14

JOE

GRABBED ON TO MY BROTHER'S ARM AND HE grabbed on to mine, both of us frozen with terror as we crawled out of the rubble into the land of the dead.

Disembodied skulls seemed to be pushing their way out of the walls all around us. Fighting living bad guys was hard enough; I had no idea how to fend off an army of dead ones. It took me another panicked minute to realize these particular dead people weren't on the attack.

"We're in the Catacombs!" Frank exclaimed.

The chamber before us wasn't just filled with bones, it was made of them. Thousands of bodies must have been stashed down there, their ancient skulls neatly embedded in walls and pillars made entirely of stacked skeleton bits.

"This must be one of the secret sections of the original

Catacombs," Frank said as he caught his breath. He'd gone so pale he looked like a ghost himself! "They moved the bodies into mass underground tombs like this one in the 1700s after they dug up all the graves when the cemeteries got too full and started to cave in. Only a small part of the Catacombs are still open to the public, though. Most of them were closed off and forgotten about years ago."

"I'm just glad it's full of old bones and not actual ghouls," I said.

"Um, Joe . . ." My brother's voice quivered as he pointed across the chamber. "I think you may have spoken too soon."

I followed his finger to the wall by the arched stone doorway—where the eyes of a cracked yellow skull began to glow bright red.

"Ahh . . ." A scream welled up in my throat, but it didn't get far. "Hey, that looks a lot more like an LED light than an evil zombie light."

I crept cautiously closer and looked deep into the skull's eyes. This time the skull really did look back—or at least the tiny spy camera hidden inside did.

"It's a Skull-Cam!" I peered in at the palm-size remote control camera. "And that's a low battery warning light, not an undead eyeball. Somebody's watching, and I'm pretty sure he isn't from the beyond."

We gave the chamber a closer inspection. Our suspect was long gone, but it was clear from the Skull-Cam and the oil-filled lanterns hanging on the wall nearby that someone had been using these tunnels regularly.

"The old lanterns make sense down here," I observed. "You don't have to worry about batteries, bulbs, or corrosion."

"Got a match?" Frank asked, grabbing one of the lanterns. "Might as well save the batteries on our phones as well."

"Good call," I replied, looking down at my phone, where I now had a low battery warning of my own to go along with the no-service icon at the top of the screen. It figured there wouldn't be any cell phone signal this far underground. Suddenly visiting the catacombs with a police chaperone seemed a lot more desirable, but we couldn't even call for one if we wanted to. We'd come this far, though, and I wasn't about to turn back.

I pulled out the little emergency kit with strike-anywhere matches I always carry with me and lit our lanterns. Casting a glance back at the Skull-Cam, I stepped through the doorway to whatever lay beyond.

"Stay alert," I whispered. "We know someone is watching."

The doorway led to an underground crossroads with three different tunnels, although it wasn't hard to figure out which one we were looking for: the one where the walls, bones and all, were covered in Ratatouille's artwork.

"I think we just found Les Ratacombes," I said, thinking about the vandalized Catacombs sign from the Georges St. Denis photograph at Cyril's house.

"I never thought a rat's nest could look so cool," Frank mused.

We stepped inside past a rainbow of decorated skulls, swirling graffiti, and floor-to-ceiling murals. Stenciled on the scary-looking door at the end of the tunnel was a life-size dancing Ratatouille skeleton.

The door had been left open just a crack. And there was something thumping on the other side.

CORNERED RAT

15

FRANK

THUMP-THUMP-THUMPTHUMPTHUMP-THUMPTHUMP-THUMP-THUMP.

A shiver shot down my spine as I tried to imagine what might be making the noise. Listening closer, I could hear the sound of muffled moans as well, which definitely didn't make me feel any better.

Joe put his finger to his lips and blew out his lantern. I did the same and crept alongside him toward the eerie blue light spilling out of the cracked door. Very slowly, we peered around the edge into a cluttered catacomb chamber turned art studio. The dim blue light was coming from a small TV screen playing the wireless video feed from the Skull-Cam. And the thumping? That came from the person watching it.

Because the person was tied to a chair, gagged, and frantically trying to free himself.

"It looks like someone already caught Ratatouille for us," Joe whispered as Georges St. Denis hopped around helplessly in the chair.

He stopped hopping when he heard Joe and jerked his head toward the door, a look of sheer terror in his eyes. Terror turned to relief when he saw us, and he immediately started trying to talk frantically through the gag. We couldn't understand a word he was saying, but the meaning was obvious. He wanted us to untie him.

"Not gonna happen, Georges," I whispered.

"If we remove the gag, will you stay quiet?" Joe asked.

"And are we alone?" I added.

He nodded so vigorously I thought he might give himself whiplash. I nodded at Joe to untie the gag. He must have had a different interpretation of the word "quiet," though, because he started gibbering uncontrollably in French the instant his mouth was free.

My French was *comme ci comme ça*—that means "okay"— but it was nowhere near good enough for me to translate the stream of rapid-fire panic spewing out of Georges St. Denis's mouth.

"How about a little slower, in English," I said, knowing he was fluent in our language from the conversation we'd overheard at the gallery.

"You must let me go! You must!" he begged.

"We're not letting you go anywhere, Rat-Man," Joe stopped him. "Not until you tell us why you stole Napoléon's pen and framed Le Stylo."

That clammed him up quickly.

"I guess we should put the gag back in, huh, Joe?" I suggested.

"*Non, non, non, s'il vous plaît!* Please don't! I can't take it anymore!" he pleaded.

"Then you better start talking," Joe told him.

He sagged in the chair.

"It is not fair," he whined quietly.

"And framing someone else for your crime so you can get away with stealing a historical artifact?" I shot back.

"I was the first one in school to discover the art of the street, and Cyril stole it from me like he steals all his ideas," he snarled. "He likes so much for his Le Stylo to take credit for others' inspiration, I simply gave him credit for what he truly is. A thief!"

"Street art doesn't belong to any one person. It's an artistic movement," Joe argued. "Le Stylo's using it as a tool for social activism to help other people, not trying to profit from it like you are."

"Social activism, ha! It is easy to pretend to care about the welfare of others when you have all the money in the world. He is able to buy his way to fame simply because he's rich, while the true artists like myself are forced to eke out a living in the gutters, like, like . . ." Georges struggled to find the right word, so my brother helped him out.

"A rat?" Joe offered.

"Yes, like a rat!" he said proudly. "They are nature's most industrious animals. They thrive in every environment even as they are persecuted unjustly and forced to survive on the scraps of those who do not appreciate their true beauty."

"From what we've heard, Cyril was giving you a lot more than just scraps. He was the biggest supporter of your photography. He even got you a show right along Le Stylo at one of the biggest galleries in Paris, and you turned around and betrayed him."

"Like a rat," Joe affirmed.

"How do you think it felt living off the handouts of an inferior artist?" he snapped. "A few thousand euros here and there is like pocket change to him. He could have driven up the prices of my work like he does his own. No one would have paid a thousand euros for one of Le Stylo's supposed masterpieces, let alone a hundred thousand, had the oh-so-wealthy art collector Cyril Brune not outbid himself to snatch them up at ridiculous prices."

I could tell we weren't going to get anywhere trying to convince Georges that what he'd done was wrong. There was no longer any doubt who the thief was, but a large chunk of the mystery still remained unsolved.

"Only you saw right through Cyril's art collector facade,"

I offered. Sometimes massaging a criminal's fragile ego was the best way to get straight answers.

"From the start! He thought he was so clever. All our other classmates fell for his little charade, but not I!" he boasted. "Cyril was never very good, but he did have passion, that I will admit. And the passion of an artist cannot simply be extinguished by a little discouragement like a weak flame in the breeze. The idea that he would never pick up a brush again was laughable. Once Le Stylo's work began to appear on the streets of Paris, I recognized the style immediately. And do you know why I recognized it?"

"No, but I have a feeling you're going to tell us," Joe mumbled.

Georges didn't even wait for Joe to finish before answering his own question. "I recognized it because I introduced him to it! Those simple two-dimensional stencils for which he is now so well-known are merely imitations of the street artists from England and America whose work I shared with my classmates. For me it was merely inspiration from which I evolved a new style all my own once I invented Ratatouille, but Cyril was obsessed. As soon as my old classmate began paying outrageous prices for a new artist named Le Stylo, I knew he'd simply rebranded his own tired artistic imitation under a new name. Then he got lazy. He became so sure no one suspected, it was easy to observe him and learn his secrets."

"I bet the high-powered drone helped too," Joe suggested.

I really liked Cyril, and the critique of his alter ego's artwork stung because it was partially true. But even Cyril himself had been honest with us about his limitations as an artist. There was something else that made his art special.

"His style may not be the most original," I conceded, "but the bold way he installs his work in places no one else would imagine, to call attention to issues that are important to him, that shows real vision."

"And courage," Joe added. "Unlike you and the selfish way you use Ratatouille's work to brag to yourself about how smart you think you are."

As if to prove Joe's point about courage, Georges suddenly turned ghostly pale and began to whimper. I followed his frightened gaze to the TV monitor showing the feed from the Skull-Cam. We'd been so intent on getting the truth out of Georges, we'd neglected to ask possibly the most important question: Why was he tied up?

The answer had just stepped onto the screen.

Simone.

And the object in her hand wasn't a pen.

It was a gun.

JOE

SHE'S GOING TO TORTURE ME INTO telling where the pen is! You have to untie me!" Georges begged as Simone walked across the screen followed by my least favorite security guard, Ginormo Luc, headlamps lighting their way.

"I think we may have overlooked a minor detail," Frank murmured.

"Did Simone figure you out or were you working for her the whole time?" I demanded.

"No! Yes! Sort of!" he said in a panic. "It was my idea. I knew she was bitter that Le Stylo made her give her commissions to charity, so I proposed to her a way to even the score. She gave me the money to bankroll the hoax at the Louvre and the heist of Napoléon's pen from Plouffe."

"And you double-crossed her," Frank accused.

"I wasn't going to, but . . ." Georges looked away like he was ashamed. "Why does she need more money? Gallery owners like her are the reason true artists like myself starve in obscurity while commercial hacks like Le Stylo get richer. Now please untie me. She will be here any minute."

"He has a point about that last part," Frank gulped. "And she has a gun."

He ran over to the door and gulped a second time. "And the door doesn't have a lock."

"I never needed one before," Georges squeaked.

The door was the only exit I could see, and there was no way to use it without running right into her in the tunnels.

"Is there another way out of here?" I asked as I searched the room in vain.

"There is a chute hidden in the corner behind the stencils," he said. "It circles back to the chamber where the camera is. Please take me with you."

I exchanged a look with my brother. Georges was a crook, but we couldn't just leave him there to be tortured.

"Check out the chute," I told Frank. "I'll cut Rat-Man from the chair."

Georges gasped as I grabbed a utility knife from a cup full of paintbrushes and pencils on the shelf next to the TV.

"Stop your squirming, I'm not going to hurt you," I assured him as I got to work sawing through the thick cord.

"Keep his hands tied," Frank cautioned, hurrying over

to the wall and shoveling stencils and pieces of poster board aside.

Sure enough, there was a perfectly round human-size hole in the floor right where Georges said. Frank stepped forward to get a closer look.

"It's totally dark. I can't see any . . . AHHHHHHHH!"

And that's when he slipped on a femur and went tumbling headfirst into darkness.

MIGHTIER THAN THE SWORD

17

FRANK

DID MY BEST NOT TO SCREAM AS I PLUM-
meted down the narrow stone chute.

"Oomph," I oomphed at the surprisingly soft landing about six feet below.

I turned my phone back on and tapped the flashlight app. I'd never been so happy to see a bunch of cardboard and canvas. The stencils and discarded paintings that fell down the chute with me had broken my fall. I may have slipped on someone else's thigh bone, but luckily, I hadn't broken my own.

Unluckily, I could hear Simone enter the room above before Joe and Georges had a chance to follow me through the chute. I couldn't see anything looking back up the chute, but Simone's voice carried clearly into the tunnel below.

"This is a rather impressive school project you've gotten yourself into." Simone laughed cruelly. "How nice of you to wander right into my trap. Now I have a rat and a mouse in one cage."

"You did not suspect the cats were lurking in another tunnel waiting to pounce," Luc's deep voice rumbled from above.

"It was you with the drone? I wouldn't have thought you could handle such a high-tech device," Joe shot back.

I could hear Luc's voice rumble again.

"Where is your brother, little mouse?" Simone said. "Luc saw you both exit the stationery shop through the drone's camera. We were expecting to catch Le Stylo, but perhaps a pair of nosy so-called art students will lead us to him."

"He, uh, he went back for the police," Joe bluffed. "They'll be here to arrest you any minute."

There was an agonizing moment of silence as Simone considered my brother's threat.

"Then we had better make Georges talk quick," she finally replied. "Unless, of course, he wants to be a good little rat and tell me where he hid Napoléon's golden pen without coercion."

"I—I—I—" Georges stammered. "I lost it."

"You spent thousands of my money to steal a million-euro gold pen, and then you lost it?" Simone hissed. "That is very unfortunate for you. Luc, retrieve the knife from the boy. Start with his painting hand."

"No!" Georges screamed.

"Not a chance," Joe said calmly. My brother's bravery made my heart beat even faster. It was up to the law to punish Georges, not Simone—but sometimes standing up for justice is dangerous business.

"Don't make me shoot you, boy," Simone said.

"Fraud, larceny, and kidnapping are bad enough. Do you really want to add shooting a teenager to the list?" Joe asked, stalling for time.

"Kidnapping." She laughed. "I was perfectly happy to help Georges get rich off Plouffe's pen until he got greedy."

"You already profited from selling the pen to Plouffe. It is not fair you get to sell it twice," Georges whined, using his own twisted logic.

"What's fair is me evening the score with Le Stylo for robbing me of my commissions. That's what you proposed to me, remember? We had a deal. I front the money, you steal the pen, I fence it on the black market, and, to borrow an American expression"—I could just see her pausing to sneer at my brother—"we both 'make out like bandits.'"

"You had a deal with Le Stylo too. A legal one," Joe reminded her.

"He can give away all his money if he wants to, whoever he is, but why should he make me give up mine?" Simone shot back. "Le Stylo would still be a nobody street artist like

Ratatouille here if it weren't for the exposure my gallery gave his work. He owes me."

"You really don't know who Le Stylo is? Georges didn't tell you?" Joe blurted.

"No, though I have a feeling you might," she said. "That was him you were visiting on Rue du Moulin Vert, was it not?"

"Thanks for the drone, by the way, Ratty," Luc interjected. "You were so busy spying on Le Stylo, you never noticed me spying on you this morning. I knew just where to fly your drone once we tied you up. If you weren't going to tell us who Le Stylo was, I knew how I could find out. Looks like you're not so smart after all."

"Whoa, Luc!" Joe laughed. "I didn't know you had that long of a speech in you!"

Luc's growl vibrated through the ceiling.

"I'm just impressed you didn't get stuck climbing through the rubble to get down here," Joe taunted Simone's enormous henchman.

I could hear the cold snap of a switchblade flicking open, followed by Luc's voice. "You can keep your little knife, boy. I brought my own."

"I'd think twice about that if I were you," Joe said. "The police are on the way, and things will go a lot worse for you if you're caught torturing someone when they get here."

"He is right," Simone agreed, and my heart lightened. But only for a second. "Maybe we should just eliminate the boy so there are no witnesses and take Georges with us."

I choked back a gasp. This time Joe's bluff had backfired. His life was in danger, and I was the only one who could help him. But how?

"Or you could bring him with us. Then there would be no bodies to leave behind," Georges suggested timidly.

"The rat has a point," Ginormo responded.

Wow, one point for Georges! But that still didn't leave me with any options. They were about to be on the move, and I didn't have a clue how to stop them. Even if I had gone back for the police, they never would have made it in time. I looked at the chute in the ceiling above me. There was no way to crawl back up. It wasn't like I could defend us anyway; the only weapon I had was the little Swiss Army knife I carried in my pocket.

But there had to be a way out of this. I just needed to calm down and think rationally. Joe would be okay. At least that's what I hoped.

I looked at the pile of cardboard and canvas lying on the floor. The first Ratatouille stencil we'd seen when we arrived in Paris looked uselessly back at me. Little good a cardboard cutout of a human-size rat carrying a baguette would do me against a gun and a switchblade.

"Fine, but we'll have to tie him up. Where did you put the rope?" I heard Simone ask Luc. A lot of confused shuffling followed.

The stencil passed through the beam of my flashlight as I

tossed it aside in frustration, casting a shadow of Ratatouille's life-size silhouette on the catacomb wall. And that's when it hit me. Maybe all this cardboard would help!

I pulled out my Swiss Army knife, flipped open the little scissors, grabbed the stencil of Ratatouille, and started cutting as I ran.

I had heard a lot of shuffling and angry French words as I left my hiding spot. Hopefully the rope was lost. I needed all the help I could get.

Georges had said the chute circled back to the chamber with the Skull-Cam, and a couple of minutes later I was standing about twenty feet from the entrance. Staying far enough away so that my phone wouldn't show up on camera, I flicked my flashlight on and off to see if it worked.

It wasn't a masterpiece, but it would have to do. I just had to hope I wasn't too late.

I turned off the flashlight and crept toward the chamber door. Standing out of view of the Skull-Cam, I propped my phone against the wall and turned the flashlight back on so the light spilled into the room. I then slowly walked the stencil through the flashlight beam, causing its shadow to move across the chamber wall right in front of the camera.

As nervous as I was about Joe, I couldn't help grinning at my handiwork.

The five-foot-tall stencil had become a shadow puppet. Only it was no longer the silhouette of a giant rat in a beret carrying a loaf of bread. It was a policeman in a French officer's cap carrying a gun that walked past the Skull-Cam.

My idea had worked! Now I just had to hope that Simone and Luc were watching the Skull-Cam monitor—and that the distraction would buy Joe time to improvise an escape. I didn't have to wait long to find out the first part.

The boom of Simone's pistol ripped through the stale air, echoing off the Catacomb walls from the direction of Georges' lair. It was followed by a scream.

VIVE LES HARDYS
18

JOE

THINGS HAD BEEN GOING PRETTY well until the gun went off.

My bluff about Frank going for the police bought Georges and me time, and I'd gotten a full confession from Simone in the process. If we managed to get out of the Catacombs alive, I'd be able to provide plenty of evidence to clear Le Stylo's name and send Simone, Luc, and Georges to the French slammer.

I was itching to know where Georges had hidden Napoléon's golden pen, but I wasn't about to let Luc torture him in order to find out. So I did my best to keep Simone talking while Georges mostly just sat there blubbering. He wasn't only blubbering, though. He also kept casting nervous glances at the shelf with the Skull-Cam monitor every time someone mentioned the pen. The third time, I realized it wasn't the TV monitor he was looking at. It was the cup next to it with the brushes, markers, and pencils. The one I'd grabbed the utility knife from.

Simone hadn't noticed, so I did my best not to let her catch me staring. She had just flipped the script on me and threatened to "eliminate" me when I finally realized why Georges had been so preoccupied with the cup. One of the drawing utensils in the cup didn't quite fit in with the black pencils, colored markers, and paint-stained brushes. And this one was pristine gleaming gold.

Like with Georges and his secret alter ego, Ratatouille, the truth was hidden in plain sight; you just had to know where to look.

And at that moment what both Simone and Luc were looking at was the shadow of an armed police officer stalking across the Skull-Cam screen.

"They're here!" Luc cried.

I had no idea how Frank could have gone for help so quickly, but I did know I might not get a better shot to keep myself alive. With my captors distracted by the cop on the Skull-Cam, I made my move. I dove for Simone's gun.

"Look out!" Luc shouted.

She raised the gun and pulled the trigger at the exact same moment I went to slap it out of her hand.

BANG!

The handgun sounded like a cannon blast inside the underground chamber.

TWANG!

The bullet ricocheted off the wall.

"AHHHHH!"

Someone screamed.

Was it me? I tried to stay calm as I felt for the gunshot wound, adrenaline surging through me, my heading ringing from the sound of the blast. It was only when I saw Luc collapse to the floor clutching his foot that I realized the bullet had hit him and not me!

I scrambled to the floor and knocked the gun out of Simone's reach. She rushed for the door, her headlamp illuminating Les Ratacombes as she sprinted for the underground crossroads that led back to the surface. I sprinted after her.

My heart leaped when I saw Frank racing toward her from the other direction.

"Stop her!" I yelled.

He was about to when the light from her headlamp caught him right in the eye. He shielded his eyes, trying to block the blinding glare. Simone took advantage of the distraction and shouldered her way past him, knocking him into the wall before he could recover.

Frank was still blinking away the spots when I caught up to him.

"I'm glad you're not dead!" he said.

"Me too!" I agreed, pulling him along after me. "Where are the police? I saw them on the Skull-Cam."

"Right there." He pointed at the stencil of the policeman lying in the doorway. It only took me a second to realize how he'd tricked us with his shadow puppet police raid.

"Good thinking, bro! That's the best art installation I've seen yet," I cheered as we ran back through the chamber to the hole in the rubble pile blocking the entrance into the sewer.

When we made it through the crawl space into the sewer tunnel, Simone was already climbing up the ladder. We dashed through the tunnel and scrambled up after her.

I poked my head out of the sewer in time to see Simone running down the alley toward the street. She was just a few feet from the intersection when a pedestrian turned the corner, accidentally blocking her path. Simone tried to put on the brakes, but it was too late. She slammed right into the startled man, knocking them both to the ground.

"Watch where you're going, lady," the pedestrian grumbled in a familiar voice as they struggled to disentangle themselves.

I realized why I recognized the voice as we ran toward them. It wasn't a pedestrian. It was Chief Olaf!

"Grab her, Chief! She's the thief!" I yelled.

Chief Olaf looked even more confused than usual, but he listened, gripping her wrists in a standard police hold while we caught up to them.

"Hey, Chief! Lucky we ran into you," Frank hollered as we ran up.

"Lucky, my rear! The GPS trackers on your phones went dead and I followed you to the last place they showed up. Now you better tell me what's going on," he ordered.

"Huh, I guess it's a good thing you bugged us after all. I thought we were on our own when we lost cell phone service in the sewer," I said with relief.

"Let go of me, you oaf!" Simone demanded.

"Who is this woman?" he asked.

"That's Simone Lachance, the owner of the gallery where Le Stylo's work is being displayed. She and her security guard Luc conspired with a street artist called Ratatouille to steal Napoléon's pen and frame Le Stylo for it. Only Ratatouille double-crossed them, so they kidnapped him to force him to tell them where he hid the pen," Frank ran down the facts for him.

"Lies!" Simone screeched.

"Luc's down in the Catacombs with a bullet in his foot from Simone's gun, and Georges is still tied to a chair," I added, ignoring Simone as I brought everyone up to speed on the part Frank hadn't seen. "Georges St. Denis is Ratatouille's real name."

"I know nothing about any of this!" Simone protested. "I am the one who was kidnapped by those men! I am lucky to have escaped with my life, and no thanks to these meddling schoolboys."

"Hmm, these boys may be meddlers, I'll concede that, but I've never known them to be outright liars," the chief said, keeping a cool head and a firm grip on his kicking suspect.

"This is a terrible injustice!" she shouted. "I am a very important person. If you do not let me go now, I will have you all thrown in jail for assault."

The chief gave Frank and me a hard look and then nodded. He knew us well enough to know when we were telling the truth.

"Good thing I brought these along." He pulled a long plastic zip tie from his fanny pack and zipped it tight around Simone's wrists as handcuffs. "I was ready to use them on the two of you if I found out you'd intentionally ditched those GPS trackers."

"You'll regret this, you cretin!" Simone howled.

"Ma'am, I don't know how things work in France, but in America suspects have the right to remain silent. I suggest you use it," Chief Olaf advised her.

"My lawyers will hear about this," she threatened, but she clammed up after that and stopped struggling.

"I'm sure Inspector Devereux will let you give them a call when he's ready, although I'm guessing you'll have more urgent things to discuss with them than the three of us." Chief Olaf kept a hand on her arm as he scrolled through the contacts on his phone and hit the talk button. I could hear the phone ringing and a faint "*Bonjour*" on the other end as someone answered.

The chief had on his smuggest grin when he started talking. "*Bonjour*, Inspector Devereux! This is Chief Olaf, the American policeman you called unprofessional. My young detective buddies the Hardy boys and I solved your crime for you. We've got one of your crooks in custody and the other two are waiting for you in the Catacombs where they were hiding out. You might want to bring the paramedics with you. Apparently they had a little tiff, and one of them took a bullet in the foot."

He gave Devereux our location and clicked off. "Boy, did that feel good!"

"Good work, Chief," I said. "You caught the bad guy!"

"Even if it was accidentally getting run over by her," Frank reminded us.

The chief looked like he was about to give us one of his signature growls, but started laughing instead. "I'm just happy you boys are safe."

"I wish we'd gotten Georges to tell us where the pen is," Frank lamented.

"Georges doesn't know it, but he did!" I informed him happily. "It's in the cup of brushes where I got the utility knife. I caught him looking at it when Simone was interrogating him. They must have really taken him by surprise, because he didn't even bother hiding it."

When Devereux and Inspector Livingston showed up a few minutes later with a caravan of police cars and emergency vehicles, we were able to tell them exactly whodunit, why, and where to find the missing pen.

"Fantastic detective work, lads," Inspector Livingston said once we'd summed everything up for them. "I will suggest to my superiors that Interpol give you a civilian commendation."

He turned to Devereux. "Perhaps the Paris police can do the same, Inspector."

"Perhaps," Devereux muttered bitterly. From his tone I figured "perhaps" basically meant "when baguettes fly."

Turns out *l'inspecteur* also had one more question for us before he let us go.

"Surely Le Stylo played a role in the theft as well, no?" he asked, one angry eyebrow cocked.

"Le Stylo was framed, Inspector. He didn't know anything about it," Frank said matter-of-factly before adding, "Whoever he is."

Frank and I hid our smiles. If Devereux was going to find out Le Stylo's secret identity, it wasn't going to be from us.

Chief Olaf gave us a suspicious look but didn't say anything.

"I'm not even going to ask," he mumbled on the Métro back to the hotel.

The news about how we'd cracked the case spread fast, and by the time we reached the hotel, we were practically celebrities. The IPAD attendees crowded around us, asking a million questions and hanging on every detail.

No one even seemed to notice when our famous detective dad finally arrived in Paris later that evening. The only Hardys anyone attending the international detectives conference wanted to hear about were Joe and Frank.